AF241340

The Unkindness Club

Purdy Franklin Mysteries #1

Jill Ammon Vanderwood, Franklin Grant-Illustrator

Idea Creations Press

Dedications

This book is dedicated to my childhood friend Kathy, who is deaf. You always challenged me to be better and to try harder. Also, thank you for encouraging me to write this book. I don't know which of us is more excited. To Susan, who I have lost track of over the years. Susan grew up with Polio and spent long days in Shriner's Hospital and also spent months in a body cast, but nothing stopped her from being joyful and optimistic.

JAV

I dedicate my artwork to my grandparents, mom and dad and many close friends. Thank you for inspiring me and encouraging me to keep going.

FG

Acknowledgements

I want to thank April Tribe Giauque for being a sensitivity reader for The Unkindness Club. She had many helpful insights which I used to tell this story from the perspective of a deaf girl. I also want to thank my husband Bill for being patient with me and my writing journey.

Also by

Other books for children and YA by Jill Ammon Vanderwood include:

Through the Rug series (Books 1-3):

Through the Rug Tenth Anniversary Edition

Through the Rug 2: Follow That Dog Tenth Anniversary Edition

Through the Rug 3: Charm Forrest

What's It Like, Living Green? Kids Teaching Kids, by the Way They Live

Erase the Problem of Bullying

Christmas Picture Books

The Year Santa Lost His List

Santa's Mysterious Boot: : Finding the True Spirit of Christmas

The Path You Choose series (Books 1-4),

Off Target

On the Rocks

Cheers

Keeping Secrets

and the upcoming: **Are We Twins? Purdy Franklin Mysteries #2.**

Contents

Chapter 1
This Birthday Changes Everything

"Make a wish!" said Persephone's mom.

"Make a wish, birthday girl!" said her dad.

"Hurry up, make a wish!" said her sister Tara, losing patience.

Persephone sat still at a long folding table, set up with a birthday table cloth, in her living room in front of her birthday cake. She watched the pink candles melt. Wax began dripping onto the chocolate icing. She felt anxious. *I'm turning ten, and that means I'm getting older. I need to think of the perfect birthday wish.*

Persephone's orange and white cat, Beau, wrapped himself around her, going in and out between her feet. She could feel him purring, which helped to calm her. For a moment, she closed her eyes and felt herself purring along with her cat. Opening her eyes, she looked around to see if anyone had noticed. Her grandmother winked at her from across the room, but everything else seemed to be normal in her living room.

Her friends, Lydia, Scarlet, and Brook, all blonds, seemed eager to help with her wish and started making suggestions. Persephone faced her friends as they spoke.

"Wish for a lot of money!" said one.

"No, wish to be magic!" said another.

She glanced over at her older twin sisters. With hands on their hips, they rolled their hazel eyes at her. Her teenage sisters, Tara and Kara, were tall with auburn hair like their dad, while Persephone had emerald, green eyes and was small for her age, with darker hair and features like her Hispanic mama.

Her sisters usually called her a pest and told her, 'Get out of our room!' But just that morning, they had *invited* her into their room and given her snacks to eat while Tara combed and curled Persephone's black hair with a natural white streak. Kara had placed a tiara on her head to make her feel special for her birthday. *They hardly ever treat me so nice. I can't wait to grow up so my sisters won't think I'm such a baby.*

Persephone had dressed in her pink princess dress with ruffles and bows, but she still wore her worn-out, pink, high-top sneakers.

Multicolored balloons got loose from their ties on the backs of chairs, some hitting the ceiling. A piñata hung from a wooden beam near the ceiling.

Persephone's parents walked stealthily around the table, removing paper plates with half-eaten slices of pizza.

"I, I wish. . ."

Persephone looked around the room, trying to decide on her wish. Her eyes fell on her white, upright piano. Persephone started learning to play the piano before becoming deaf from meningitis at age six. She continued learning to play by memorization and the feel of the music's vibrations.

"I could wish to be a famous pianist," Persephone said aloud.

"Wait, I need to wish silently, right?"

"Yes, yes," said her sister Kara. "Make a wish already!"

"Okay, I will," said Persephone, throwing up her hands.

The other night, she'd dreamed she was riding on a unicorn.

That's it! I wish my dreams would come true.

"I made my wish, so now I can blow out the candles," she said aloud.

Persephone who blew out all ten candles with one big breath, took another breath and said,"Now everyone gets cake and ice cream!"

She watched as the group of friends and family let out their breath in a collective sigh.

Everyone seemed to be speaking at once, and Persephone could only pick out part of their conversations by reading lips. She turned toward her mama as she said, "I bought --- cakes. One--- ----------- icing --- --- with vanilla.

She turned toward her dad, and he was saying, "Don't --- them——right now. Wait—see ---- ---- of ---- wants."

She turned to Grandma. --- you ----this----- too ---- ---------- ---- her?"

Her three blond friends were playing a clapping game and moving around so fast she could hardly keep up, "---- Mary Black ---- all ------- in ----- black."

Her sisters were also talking, and Rowen was trying to get her attention by tapping her on the shoulder. Things got so loud in her living room that Persephone, who relied on hearing aids, could no longer make out individual voices or conversation. She covered her ears and ran from the room.

Her redheaded friend Rowen followed her in his motorized wheelchair. "What's wrong, Persephone?"

"I'm having trouble with all the noise." She removed her hearing aids from behind each ear and turned down the volume one at a time before placing them back in her ears.

Mama cut the cake and served it to the partygoers while Grandma, sensing the problem, encouraged the group to quiet down before the birthday girl returned.

Persephone and Rowen came back to the living room. She seated herself at the table while Rowen rolled up beside her. Mama placed a piece of cake with ice cream in front of each of them.

Grandma, Mama, Dad, her sisters, and friends excitedly rushed to get their presents for her to open.

She pushed her cake aside and opened gifts of new clothes, as well as a new pair of pink high-top sneakers to replace the worn-out pair she still wore. She then opened a new suitcase for trips to Grandma's house, a box of chocolate candy, mystery books, a Target gift card, plus thirty-five dollars in cash. But her favorite gift, from her parents, was a pet gerbil in a cage with a water bottle, a small ladder and a running wheel.

"I'm going to name my new pet Cookie," said Persephone.

"She kind of looks like a cookie," said Mama.

"Yeah," said Kara. "She's tan, like a peanut butter cookie."

"Just don't eat her; she's a pet, not a cookie," said Dad, jokingly.

Everyone laughed, but Persephone began to meow. Her green eyes went wide, and she quickly covered her mouth with her arm. Her grandmother paid particular attention, but no one else seemed to notice.

Persephone thanked her guests and set her gifts aside.

Next, they lined up to take turns hitting the piñata hanging from the ceiling. Rowen went first, using a broom handle to hit the piñata. He made a tiny hole, making it easier for the other kids to break it open.

Persephone picked up an armful of candy and piled it on Rowen's lap.

Rowen tapped her on the arm to get her attention and then said, "Whoa, Persephone, you're giving me too much." He filled a few small bags with candy and gave the rest back to her.

Soon, the party came to an end, and parents arrived to pick up their kids.

"Thank you all for coming," said Mama, speaking with her Spanish accent, and signing. "If you don't mind, we could use your help cleaning up."

Persephone and her friends grabbed trash bags and chipped in to clear the room of cups, plates, discarded wrapping paper, and remnants of the broken piñata.

Persephone had fun at her party but, after her guests left, she enjoyed the quiet living room without the extra noise being picked up by her hearing aids. She fed Cookie lettuce leaves for half an hour before her mother reminded her not to feed her so much.

Her dad carried her new pet to her room and situated the cage on the floor, below her bedroom window.

Later that evening, Persephone thought about her fun birthday as she went sleepily to the bathroom to brush her teeth. She then headed toward her bedroom.

On her way, Persephone peeked into her parents' room to say good-night. Her mom motioned for her to enter the room and take a seat on the corner of the bed. Persephone absentmindedly opened and closed her hands, then began licking one closed fist. Color started at her neck and rose to her cheeks. She looked at her hands in disbelief. *Why would I lick my hand like that?*

Persephone quickly sat on the hand she'd licked, avoiding the temptation to do it again.

Chapter 2
Braving the Darkness

Her mother didn't seem to notice her daughter's strange behavior. She hugged Persephone and spoke English with a Spanish accent, using both words and sign language, which the family learned together after Persephone became deaf.

"Good night, sweetheart. Happy birthday! Your dad and I love you very much! I hope this day was special for you." She finger-combed Persephone's hair away from her face, revealing the two behind-the-ear hearing aids. Mama kissed her cheek and said, "I can't believe our youngest daughter is already ten. You're growing up so fast!"

Persephone stood, looked herself over, opened her emerald eyes wide, and said, "I don't think I'm growing up very fast. I still look the same as I did yesterday."

Her mama wore her own black hair in a long braid down her back. She giggled, then said, "You'll see. You *are* growing up!"

"Mama, now that I'm ten, I want to try sleeping without my night-lights."

Mama spoke to Persephone's dad, who peeked in from the attached bathroom, still brushing his teeth, "Persephone is learning to be coura-geous!"

Her dad finished brushing his teeth and joined them in the bed-room. "She's ten years old, growing up, *and* being brave! I think this birthday changes everything."

Persephone giggled, but what was that? She thought she heard her cat meow, but Beau wasn't around. She could often pick up higher frequency sounds with her hearing aids, like a cat's meow, but not the lower growl of a dog.

Could that sound be coming from me?

"Oh, you silly girl! Trying to sound like a cat!" said Dad.

Unsure what to think about the sound she'd made for the second time, she hugged each parent and left their room. Persephone was tired when she reached her two-tone, pink bedroom. She switched on the overhead light and checked on Cookie. She turned on the bedside lamp before removing all five nightlights. Persephone turned off the overhead light, sat on her full-sized bed, and didn't even get into her pajamas. She lay down on her flowered comforter and looked at the digital clock. It was 9:00 p.m.

Persephone switched off the bedside lamp and quickly closed her eyes.

If I fall asleep quickly, I won't notice how dark my room has become.

Chapter 3
The Transformation of Persephone Franklin

Cat

Persephone woke abruptly and looked around. The clock read 10:00 p.m., so she had been asleep only briefly. Something wasn't right. Her stomach seemed to be growling, but that was not all. She felt tingly all over, and she was suddenly warm and felt *fuzzy*! *The room seems different. It's larger somehow. Even my bed feels bigger.*

Persephone's room no longer seemed so dark. Outlines and shadows spooked her momentarily. But she realized she could see in the dark, as if a light was still on somewhere. However, she remembered turning out the lights before going to sleep.

Rubbing a hand across her face and through her hair, Persephone noticed that her features had changed. And her hand didn't seem to have fingers. *I don't think I've grown up in the last hour.*

What is that warm fury feeling? Did I lie down on top of my cat? No, that can't be it. Beau would have squirmed and wiggled under me.

Persephone flailed around on her bed, and her movements seemed shorter and quicker than usual. But this movement also caused her loose-fitting clothes to fall off. And why were her fingernails scratching the blankets? When she reached to turn on the tabletop lamp, her fingers couldn't even press the button.

Her yell for help produced a vibration deep down in her throat. Since she was still deaf, but no longer wearing her hearing aids, Persephone was unsure if any sound had escaped. *Am I sick? Do I have a sore throat? It doesn't seem painful.*

Persephone tried to stand up but sprang from the bed instead. It was a long way to the floor, but she landed softly. When she got down, she walked on all four *hands*. Or did she have four feet? No, instead, she saw four tiny, white paws!

Standing on her *back* legs and stretching out as tall as possible, Persephone couldn't even reach the light switch she had turned off before going to bed.

I know I'm still in my bedroom, but who am I? If Mama thinks I'm growing up so fast, then why do I seem so much smaller? I never saw my parents or sisters go through changes like this!

The door to Persephone's room was closed. Her lights wouldn't turn on, and she hadn't pulled back the covers on her bed, but her newfound, changed hands wouldn't even do that. Unable to get over how small and *furry* she was, Persephone looked into the full-length mirror on her closet door. With the help of her improved vision and the streetlight shining through her open curtain, the face she saw, the feet, the whiskers, and the tail were those of a cat. Her emerald eyes became large circles, and she jumped back quickly from the fright of what she saw in the mirror. She stood back and studied the mirror from a distance. *Wait, I have a tail? I am a cat!*

Through the mirror, she spotted the gerbil cage with her pet Cookie running on the wheel. Persephone pictured her gerbil between two slices of white bread. She crouched down and crept along the floor toward the gerbil cage, her mouth watering. Persephone stopped herself mid-pounce.

No, wait, what am I doing? I can't even think about eating Cookie! No, no, no, this is ridiculous! She shook her head so hard that spit from her mouth flung around the room.

Astonished by this new transformation, many words and sounds played in her head. *What's happening? Ahhhh! EEEYAAA! AARRGH! Holy Cow!* Even though she couldn't yell out, she still tried.

How does a ten-year-old girl go from being a human to a cat? Could this be happening because of my birthday wish?

Persephone wasn't sure how to jump onto her bed, so she curled into a ball with her tail wrapped around her, lay her head on the rug beside her bed, and tried to slow her breathing.

Another weird thing happened as she lay on the rug; Persephone lifted one paw to her mouth and *licked* her foot. With the wet foot, she began washing her face! *Ick, ick, ick, I just washed my face with spit!*

At last, she fell into a fitful sleep.

She could barely detect her alarm clock vibrating at 7:30 a.m. Persephone thought she must have been dreaming since she woke up as a girl, sleeping on the floor beside her bed.

There were still a few unexplainable things. Persephone usually woke with a dry mouth, but that morning her tongue was coated with black and white fur. Besides that, she was undressed, without a blanket to cover her. She turned off the alarm and grabbed her robe, hanging from a hook on her bedroom door. After putting it on, Persephone ran to the mirror—just like she had in her dream the night before. *I need to make sure.* This time, a girl, not a cat, looked back at her. *What a relief!*

"Where did I put my hearing aids?"

With the help of hearing aids, Persephone could hear certain sounds. Attending a deaf school for two years helped her learn sign language and lip-reading, which also helped her understand what people were saying.

"I'm pretty sure I forgot to remove my hearing aids before I went to sleep," she said.

She searched the top of her nightstand. She found her hearing aid charger, but they were not inside. *It's strange that I remembered to charge my phone, but not my hearing aids,* she thought to herself. She removed her phone from the charger and put it in the pocket of her robe. She checked inside both drawers of her nightstand but couldn't find her hearing aids.

Persephone picked up the rumpled, scattered clothes she had worn the day before. Then, she found a hearing aid at the bottom of her bed. She grabbed her phone and clicked on the flashlight. She then found the second one on the floor, barely under her bed.

What? How did they get there? I usually charge them overnight, but since that didn't happen, I'll need to charge them for at least thirty minutes before I go to school. While they're charging, I 'll have enough time to get dressed and eat before I leave for school.

Persephone pushed her worried thoughts away. Like any other day, she got ready for school, brushing her long hair into a high ponytail.

Why should she worry? It was only a dream.

Chapter 4
A New Normal?

Rowen Carter rode up a small incline to Persephone's two-story house, in his battery-powered wheelchair, and rang the doorbell. When Persephone opened the door, she noticed his windblown red hair and freckles standing out on his flushed cheeks.

Persephone ran up the stairs to get her hearing aids, then grabbed her backpack and joined him outside. Rowen had been in a wheelchair his whole life. He was born with spina bifida, causing damage to his spine so that he couldn't walk. Rowen didn't let his chair slow him down. Sometimes, Persephone had a hard time keeping up.

Before leaving Persephone's house, Rowen asked, "Does it feel any different to be ten years old?"

Thoughts raced through her head. She wasn't sure what to say. Was she ready to discuss the scare she had experienced the night before?

Persephone shrugged and quietly thought about it as they left her front door and headed down the sidewalk toward school.

Other kids were walking in the same direction but didn't appear to be listening to Persephone and Rowen.

She finally replied to Rowen's question. "I didn't think I felt any different until I dreamed that I was a cat."

Rowen put a hand over his mouth, trying not to giggle, but failing. "A cat! You dreamed that you were a cat?"

Some boys in front of them turned around and smirked.

Although her voice was hard to regulate with her hearing loss, Persephone tried to speak quietly, hoping that only Rowen could hear.

"Yes—and the weird thing is that I woke up sleeping on the floor without wearing any clothes!"

"Where were your clothes?" he asked loudly.

One of the boys in front of them turned around and stared at her. Persephone blushed and wished she hadn't said anything. She narrowed her emerald, green eyes, held up both hands in the shape of claws, and a deep sound started forming in her throat. She curled her upper lip and began to hiss. Then she quickly caught herself and half-hissed, half-spoke the words. "It was only a dream, dork!"

A look of disbelief crossed Rowen's face. He held his palms up in a 'what was that?' gesture and motioned that he and Persephone should cross the street.

Persephone then said, "S-h-h-h! Rowen, you didn't have to say it so loud. Do you swear you won't tell anyone? No one!"

"I won't. I swear!" Rowen said while crossing his heart. "I won't tell anyone! But this changes everything, Purrrr-sephone! From now on, I'm going to call you P-u-r-d-y. Purdy Franklin. You know, because you *purr* like a cat!"

She really didn't mind being called Purdy. She thought about the dream she'd had. But even as a girl, some of her behaviors did seem more catlike than they had before.

Chapter 5
Passing Notes

Letter

Purdy was tired all morning at school. Her mind went back and forth between her dream the night before, waking up in an embarrassing situation, talking to Rowen on the way to school, and the way she hissed and showed her 'fangs' that morning. When lunchtime came, she stood inside the cafeteria, holding her food tray, and waited for Rowen to join her.

Purdy's hearing aids were ineffective in a noisy environment, such as in a school lunchroom, so she usually turned them off before going to lunch.

She waved when she saw her friends, Lydia, Scarlett, and Brook, who came to her birthday party, seated at a table eating their lunch. They waved back and offered for her to sit next to them. She sat at the end of the bench so Rowen ride up in his chair beside her.

Purdy watched Lydia, who was very animated, speaking boldly and using hand gestures. "- ---- letter ---- night. It--- ---------- to – but ----- wasn't - ------- address.

Although Purdy could only pick out a few of the words, Lydia motioned toward a letter in a pastel pink envelope that she held in her hands. The envelope was addressed to her, but there was no stamp. Two other girls held up letters, one in a peach-colored envelope and the other in baby blue.

Purdy always carried a small recorder to class, since she could only hear part of what her teacher said. She switched it on and pushed it closer to the girls at the table.

I hope this recorder won't pick up too much background noise, so I can listen to the conversation after things quiet down.

Rowen rolled his chair up next to her, carrying his lunch tray on his lap. Purdy had her tray on the table in front of her. She held up a hand, asking him to stop. Purdy put up a finger for him to wait a minute. She then put her hand behind her ear and mouthed the word, 'Listen.'

Sometimes, Purdy could only pick up a few words from reading lips. It helped if the speaker turned toward her and didn't put a hand over their mouth. It was also helpful to have a friend like Rowen, who was listening. She had taught Rowen some sign language and hand gestures as well.

After a while, there was less talking, and the hand gestures stopped when the girls at the table formed a group huddle.

Purdy picked up her recorder from the table and switched it off. Rowen signed to Purdy that it was time to go. She picked up her tray of uneaten food. By now, they both had cold spaghetti, so they each removed their milk carton and a roll, then returned their trays.

On their way out, kids moved aside so Rowen could pass. Purdy and Rowen went by other tables where kids were holding up notes in pastel-colored envelopes that they had received.

Once they reached the hallway, Rowen pointed to the door and mouthed, "Let's go outside."

Purdy liked to go ahead of him and press the wheelchair accessible disk to open the door.

When they were outside, away from all the noise and confusion, Purdy took out her hearing aids and turned on the volume, returned them to her ears, and asked, "What is it? What did they say, Rowen?"

He said, "I missed the first part of the conversation. Will you rewind your recorder so you can listen? Then you can fill me in."

Purdy's recorder was hooked up to Bluetooth, so she could hear the messages directly from her hearing aids.

Scarlett was saying, "I can't believe you got a letter, Lydia. I got one too."

"What did your note say?" asked Scarlett.

Lydia answered, "It's a warning, telling me that they saw me take out my phone during a test, and they have pictures. It says that they will report me for cheating!"

Scarlett said, "Whoa! Whoever it was must be the real cheater. They couldn't take pictures of you unless they had their phones out, too!

"My letter says they saw me stuffing candy in my pockets at the store when I thought no one was looking—and they have pictures."

"Did you do that? Scarlett?"

"No. But when I got home from the store, I found candy in both of my coat pockets. I don't know how it got there, but I didn't steal it. At least, not intentionally!"

"Did anyone else get a note?" asked Lydia.

"I did," said Nadia. "Mine said that my parents aren't really my parents, and that they only took me because no one else wanted me!"

Nadia continued. "I was adopted as a baby. These are the only parents I have ever known, and my parents love me."

"Who wrote the notes?" asked Brook. "I don't have one, and I hope I don't get one!"

"Mine was signed, The Unkindness Club," said Lydia.

"Yeah, mine too," said Scarlett.

"Un-huh," said Nadia.

Once she had listened, she disconnected from her hearing aids and sat quietly so Rowen could hear the recordings.

When he had finished listening, Rowen suggested they make a list of everyone they knew who had received a note. "This will be helpful if we decide to help solve the mystery."

Purdy was quiet for a minute. "I'm not sure I would know *how* to solve a mystery."

"Come on, Purdy," said Rowen, using his new nickname for her. "It'll be

fun trying to figure this out!"

Chapter 6
Rowen Carter

At the end of the school day, Rowen rode home in his wheelchair beside Purdy, with hardly a word spoken between them.

Finally, Rowen spoke up, "I've also been thinking about your dream, Purdy. What's the meaning of a dream when you turn into a cat and then wake up as a girl?"

"Stop worrying about that, Rowen. It was only a silly dream," said Purdy.

"But was it only a dream, Purdy? I mean, I'm not sure after seeing your strange cat-like reaction on our way to school this morning. This might sound ridiculous, but I'm wondering if a girl *could* become a cat."

"I'm not a cat now, Rowen!" She moved her hands down her body, then up to her head. "See, I'm a girl."

"Yes, you are a girl, Pu-r-r-r-d-y! But you're a girl who acts like a cat! Remember how you hissed at some kids this morning, and put your hands into claws?" He demonstrated by making claws with his own hands.

"Yes, Rowen. You're right! You are being ridiculous!"

They reached Rowen's large gray house. Purdy said goodbye and turned to go.

"No, wait, Purdy. I've been thinking about ways we could solve the mystery of The Unkindness Club and their letters."

She nodded slowly.

"Purdy, the letters aren't coming through the mail, since they didn't use stamps. Maybe we could go out at night and watch for The Unkindness Club when they pass out letters in those colored envelopes."

"Go out at night, Rowen? In the dark? Just two kids alone? What if they're dangerous? Did you think about that?"

"Well, yeah, maybe not at night," he said.

She started to leave, once more.

Rowen rode up behind her and tapped her on the hand. "Wait, Purdy! We still have a mystery to solve."

She turned to face him. "Don't tell me you already have everything figured out. We just found out about the letters today at lunchtime."

"Well, uh, no, I haven't solved anything yet, but I want to run an experiment. I have a spy gadget I picked up from my dad's workshop. If I can test out my tracker, it could help solve this mystery."

"Will you come with me, Purdy? You don't need to say or do anything. Just follow my lead, okay?"

"Okay, Rowen. I'm in."

"Wait here. I need to drop off my backpack and grab my device."

He rode his chair up a wheelchair ramp and entered his house through the purple front door with a lower doorknob at his level. Several minutes later, Rowen reappeared. Purdy joined him outside his house and walked beside him as he maneuvered his chair back down the ramp.

Facing Purdy, he said, "My plan involves my friend Henry. Do you remember Henry? The guy who drives the delivery van for the grocery store?"

"Yes, I remember Henry. Sometimes he drives you to appointments. But what does he have to do with this mystery?"

He faced toward Purdy, shook his head, and said, "Henry doesn't have anything to do with the mystery. I'm just running an experiment. Oh, there he is. I was sure he'd be coming this way sooner or later,"

Rowen waved frantically at a passing van. The driver rolled down his window, still moving slowly.

"Hey, Henry, have you got a minute?" asked Rowen.

Henry pulled his van to the curb, stopped and jumped out.

"Hey, Rowen, Persephone!" With long legs, he climbed from the delivery van, went around to the back, and took out three grocery bags. "Give me a minute to deliver these to Mrs. Helman."

Rowen pretended to be waiting beside the van. However, when Henry had his back turned, Rowen pulled a magnetic tracking disc, the size of a quarter, from his shirt pocket.

He showed the device to Purdy before driving his chair up to the curb, close to the van. The tires were large, with wide wheel wells. Without hesitation, Rowen placed the device on the metal above the passenger-side tire. He mouthed quietly, "If this works, I can use it to spy around the neighborhood."

It was only moments before they noticed Henry heading down Mrs.

Helman's driveway and returning to his van.

"It's good to see you kids out and about. Can I drop you somewhere?"

"Yes," said Rowen, nodding. "Would you drop us off at the library? I need to pick up a book on electronic spy gadgets."

"Wait," said Purdy, "I need to let my mom know where I am."

Purdy pulled her phone out of her backpack and sent a text to her mom. She let Rowen read it.

> I'm with Rowen, we're getting a ride with Henry, the delivery guy from the store, and heading for the library. I'll be home in a few hours.

She soon felt the vibration of her mom's return text, and she showed Rowen her mom's answer.

> *Sure! See you then.*

Purdy said, "Okay, I can go."

Henry scratched his head, "Electronic spy gadgets, huh? I've known you two since you were in preschool, and you're always up to something."

He came around the vehicle and opened the passenger side door and faced her, saying, "Persephone, why don't you hop up in the front seat and buckle up? I'll turn off the airbag."

He then spoke to Rowen, "You know the drill. I'll pull out the ramp in the back of the van so you can wheel yourself in and right up to the cab."

Rowen rode through the back of the delivery van, passing bags of groceries, until Purdy saw him arrive between the two front seats.

Henry folded the ramp and closed the back doors. He got into the driver's seat.

"I'll buckle your chair to the floor, Rowen, as I've done before, so it won't move around when the van is in motion."

Henry turned toward Purdy and asked, "Didn't you move away for a while?"

Purdy signed the word 'yes' as she spoke. "Yes, I went to a deaf school for a few years so I could learn sign language and how to read lips."

She turned back to Rowen as he spoke. "Purdy is also teaching me some sign language. It's a great tool for a spy. That way we can talk to each other, and no one knows what we're saying."

Purdy agreed and turned toward Henry, who nodded his approval. "A spy, huh? What do you plan to do over the weekend?"

Purdy answered since Rowen was tracking the van's movements through an app on his phone. "We're trying to solve a mystery."

"A mystery?" asked Henry.

Rowen looked up from his phone and said, "Yep."

Purdy explained. "Several kids at school got letters from a group calling themselves The Unkindness Club."

Turning toward Purdy, Henry said, "Oh, really! What kind of letters?"

Purdy said, "Well, one girl got a note saying someone saw her stuffing candy into her pockets at the store. She said she didn't do it, but when she checked her coat pockets, someone had filled them with candy."

Purdy turned back to look at Rowen, and he said, "Another note said that a girl was cheating on a test because they had a picture of her taking out her phone."

Facing Purdy, Henry said, "So, let me get this straight. A couple of girls got notes from The Unkindness Club, and now you and Rowen want to solve the mystery?"

Purdy watched Rowen as he answered. "Henry, that's not all. We saw many others at school who received these notes."

They soon arrived at the library and said their goodbyes.

From a corner table between juvenile fiction and a magazine rack, Rowen and Purdy continued to follow the tracker from Rowen's phone. The delivery van zig-zagged up one street and down another, making stops along the way. After another forty minutes, Henry returned to the grocery store on Standon Blvd.

"Yes!" Rowen pumped his fist. "I knew this test would work!" Purdy grinned widely and signed 'yes'. A librarian scowled at him and said, "Shhhh!"

Before they left the library, Rowen found a magazine featuring all the latest spy gadgets and checked it out for two weeks.

"Rowen, I'm thinking that maybe we *can* solve this mystery!"

"Sure, we can, Purdy."

Chapter 7
Being a Cat

Cat

Once Persephone transformed into a cat for the second night, she was sure it *would* continue to happen the following night. So, on the third night, Purdy planned to follow her cat, Beau. If this was her new normal, she wanted to see what a regular cat would do at night. Before her nightly transformation, Purdy left her bedroom door open a crack so she could leave her room later. She wrote a note for her mama, in case she didn't return, and no one knew where to find her. She had never left her home alone at night before, and leaving this note seemed a little bit like asking for permission.

> *Mama, I went out to follow my cat tonight. I'm not sure where he's going.*
>
> *If I don't return by morning, please look for Beau. If you find him, you will probably find me nearby.*
>
> *Love, P.*

Purdy put her note into an envelope, licked it, and wrote *Mama* on the outside. She left the note on the nightstand beside her bed.

When the transformation began, her body seemed to shrink, her ears grew pointy on top of her head, and she grew warm, feeling fury. This transition was not painful, but she felt tingly all over. Purdy was filled with excitement and dread all at once. She thought about how fun it would be to follow her cat. But on the other hand, she was leaving the house at night. Alone. *I can't let myself think about that. I won't be alone. I'm going out with my cat.*

Purdy departed her bedroom and went softly down the polished wooden steps. The downstairs was dark, except for a light coming from the TV room. She entered the backyard through the cat door in the kitchen and noticed bright eyes in a tree.

I think that might be a squirrel or an owl watching me.

Beau was ahead of her, but she soon caught up. He went around the side of the light brick house and sniffed the trash cans.

He's probably looking for a tasty treat—yuck!

She had second thoughts when she smelled the fish they had for dinner the night before. *Funny, I never really noticed the smell of tasty fish before.*

Purdy was thinking about getting a garbage-can treat when her cat took off! Beau leaped up on the white-painted, wooden fence that separated their yard from the one next door. She looked at the fence for several minutes before trying her skills at leaping. The top of the fence seemed too high and narrow.

Here goes! If I don't make it, I'll crash into the trash cans and make a racket. And then there will be trash spilled out all over the yard!

One, two, three—go! Her legs seemed to spring up, and she landed lightly on the pointy edge of the fence, her fingernails catching on and holding her tight. *Wow, I made it! No trash was spilled, and no loud noises brought my mama outside!*

Before she could congratulate herself on a smooth landing, her cat leaped from the fence and ran down the neighbor's driveway toward the sidewalk.

I think I can learn a few things from Beau!

Next, Beau ran along the sidewalk, swishing his tail and moving his head from side to side while opening his mouth. She suspected that he was making cat sounds.

Purdy needed to speed up, or Beau would get away. As she followed, sensor lights came on in several driveways. Occasionally, a movement in the dark would startle her, and her breath would catch in her throat, but she continued following her marmalade cat.

She trailed him to an old woodpile, next to a garage at the back of a dark, abandoned property. Her path was no longer guided by streetlights. As she got closer, she saw glowing cat eyes as another cat walked out from behind a woodpile. Her marmalade cat and a smaller Siamese cat greeted each other by sniffing and then rubbing against each other.

Next, both cats disappeared behind the wood, and each came out with a tiny kitten in their mouth. Beau carried a tiny black kitten, and the mother cat carried a calico one, each holding on by its scruff.

Why, you sly old cat! You have a family! No wonder you're gone so much. But none of the kittens look anything like Beau.

The other adult cat followed Beau as he approached the weather-beaten garage. With her night vision, Purdy saw shards of glass from broken windows and missing roof shingles lying scattered on the ground. Weeds and vines surrounded the old, rickety building. Beau went in through a broken board on the side of the building and disappeared with the kitten he carried. The mother cat followed.

What could you possibly be doing in there, Beau? There's no way I'm following you into that building!

As she watched, both cats came out without the kittens and returned to the woodpile. And then, they each carried another kitten.

When the cats were on their way to deliver the next two kittens to the garage, Purdy decided to peek behind the wood. There, she saw two tan newborn kittens, their eyes weren't yet open, curled up together. Suddenly, feeling protective of this little family, she wanted to help. Purdy picked up a kitten by the scruff of the neck, using her lips, rather than her teeth, like she had seen the other cats do. This was so awkward for a girl-turned-cat. She tried not to bump the tiny creature into anything while she climbed out from the firewood. Purdy jumped down with her mouth full of the furball. She followed the path where she had seen the other cats go. Peeking her head into the opening of the garage, Purdy saw a cozy bed of leaves and an old blanket where the other kittens had curled up.

This place is so cold and damp and... Eeow! What was that?

She walked through a spider's web. The web tangled in her eyelashes and whiskers, but she still carried the kitten.

When she saw Purdy with her kitten, the mother cat looked angry with fangs showing and ready to attack. However, Beau greeted Purdy by sniffing and rubbing up against her, like he had greeted the other cat. She could feel him purring alongside her. The female cat seemed to sense that her kittens were safe, and she calmed down, curling up next to her young litter. Purdy took her tiny bundle to the blanket and gently released the kitten beside its siblings.

Beau left the garage and returned to the woodpile to carry the last kitten to the mother cat.

Purdy lay down next to the bundle of kittens. The soft kitten she had carried snuggled up against her and began vibrating as Beau had. Purdy enjoyed the closeness of the tiny creature, and her instincts kicked in. She started licking the little one and making sounds of her own, which she felt deep down in her throat. This didn't even seem yucky to her. It was soothing.

After bringing in the last kitten, Beau left again and returned, carrying a mouse, which he laid at the mother cat's feet.

Hey, it looks like he's feeding her. Beau is such a great dad!

I would never, ever eat a mouse. No, not now or ever. But . . . something is tempting about that mouse. No, no, yuck, yuck! I just threw up in my mouth!

Purdy now had a new appreciation for her cat and knew how it felt to be a cat, protecting young kittens on a cold autumn night.

I need to talk to my mom about these kittens. Maybe we could adopt one or two of them.

Chapter 8
What's going on?

Purdy left the little cat family and headed toward home, longing for her own bed.

As she approached the street, she saw two dark figures leaning against a tree. Purdy got closer and watched.

In the streetlight, she could see the face of an older girl she knew, Elenore Knight. *She's a friend of my twin sisters.* The other figure had its face turned away from Purdy. The two hooded figures didn't know it wasn't only a cat watching them; Purdy was also a girl who knew one of them.

Before the figures walked away, one of them dropped a shiny object that flashed in the light and disappeared into the grass.

I need to remember this spot so I can come back in the daylight and find the object they dropped.

Purdy couldn't hear anything as she followed behind. She watched as the hooded figures taped notes to doors around the neighborhood.

She got close to one residence, but as a small cat, she couldn't read the name on the envelope from the high spot where it was posted on the door. Then she got lucky. One loose note fluttered to the ground. Purdy read from the sidewalk.

> *Mrs. Clemmons,*
>
> *It is not okay to cut through your neighbor's yard. You say you're looking for your cat, but I saw you looking through your neighbor's windows. I have been following you. You are a Peeping Tom, Mrs. Clemmons. I have pictures, and I will report you to the authorities.*
>
> *The Unkindness Club.*

Hey, thought Purdy, *This is the same kind of letter they sent to kids at my school. Maybe Rowen and I can find out who's calling themselves The Unkindness Club and why they're doing this. I already have a few clues. For one, I saw a girl I know.*

It may take a good spy to bring down a bad spy.

After the two dark figures left, Purdy continued home. When she got to her neighbor's yard, she leaped onto the fence again and gently jumped onto the walkway leading to her two-story home. No lights were on inside the house, but a sensor light lit up the yard. Purdy went through the cat door into the kitchen, through the living room, and swiftly up the stairs, stopping in front of her bedroom door.

The door must have closed since I left the room earlier. Now, it's barely open a crack. With her tiny paws and short cat arms, it took great effort to open the crack wide enough for Purdy to squeeze through. She looked at the digital clock on her nightstand. The glowing red letters let her know that it was nearly 2:00 a.m. She was tired.

When Persephone's vibrating alarm clock went off at 7:30 a.m., she woke up as a girl and could hardly make herself move. *If I spend my nights being a cat, I need to start taking cat naps during the day.* She also noticed that her mouth was extremely dry. *My tongue is coated with baby cat fur.*

Chapter 9
The Shiny Object

P urdy could hardly get her mind off the shiny object she saw falling to the ground when she was a cat, the previous night. What she thought was a clue may only have been a candy wrapper. She had to find out. Purdy still hadn't gotten up the courage to tell Rowen that she was a cat, but now she needed his help searching for the lost object.

How could she tell him about the object without telling him she turned into a cat each night around 10 p.m.? And would he even believe her?

The following day after school, she told Rowen, "I decided to follow my cat, Beau, last night, and I saw two dark figures passing out *unkindness* notes."

"Purdy, you followed your cat *at night*?"

She shrugged and said, "Yeah! I'll explain later, but now we should look for clues. The Unkindness Club didn't notice me, but I saw my sister's friend, Elenore."

"Hey, Purdy! You already found a clue, and you know one of the club members. That's great!" said Rowen.

"I know! I'm excited about solving this mystery, Rowen. If you can help me now, we might find another clue. One of the dark figures dropped something shiny last night, so we need to find out what it is."

"That's terrific, Purdy. Where do you think they dropped it?"

"Follow me."

The two spy kids reached the grassy area near the corner where Purdy thought the object had been dropped, but things looked different in the daylight. Trying to think about the direction she was coming from and the direction she'd headed toward home. She figured she was either on Elm Street or possibly Piper Street.

She also remembered that not only was it dark the night before, but... But she was a cat at the time. *Cats seem to know directions. But how could a cat read a street sign from a low position? Well, I guess most cats can't read, so that wouldn't be a problem.*

Then she remembered the fallen note, addressed to Mrs. Clemmons, her former piano teacher. "Hey, I know!" said Purdy. She hurried to the corner facing her teacher's home. Rowen followed, going up the curb ramp and staying on the sidewalk. "It was here!" She pointed to the grassy area near the corner. "The note dropped over there. Elenore and the other person were standing next to that tree, over there," she said, pointing to a large tree. They were facing in this direction, so the object dropped a-r-o-u-n-d here, and it either bounced or... dropped into the grass, which would be right around here." Purdy walked around and ended up on a spot of grass where she figured the object had landed.

Rowen faced Purdy and asked, "Are you sure you weren't dreaming again?"

"No. No, Rowen, I wasn't dreaming!" She rolled her emerald eyes at the very thought. "If I were dreaming, then that means I was sleep-walking, and I'm sure I was awake, and so were The Unkindness Club members. I'm positive it was right around here, Rowen."

Rowen couldn't help Purdy search the ground from his wheelchair seat, but he could help in other ways. He pulled a monocular from his pocket. It was like binoculars but had a single lens for one eye.

Seeing the look of surprise on Purdy's face, he said, "A monocular is a tool that every spy should have."

Purdy kicked the grass, hoping to see something. She then got down on her hands and knees and crawled around. Rowen wheeled along the sidewalk near her and searched around the edges of the grass with his spy tool. He waved his hand to get her attention, then, facing her, he said, "I see something over there, Purdy. It could be a coin or a ring."

She crawled over to where Rowen was pointing. "I can only see candy wrappers. I think someone was standing here eating candy. There is one, two...five Werther candy wrappers in this area."

She focused on Rowen when he said, "Okay, pick up the wrappers. I know you'll see it once they're out of the way."

Purdy stuck the candy wrappers into her pocket and kept looking. "Yes, here it is, Rowen! It's mostly round, but it's not a coin or a ring. It's a medal on a chain. It must have fallen off someone's neck. Hey, let me borrow your monocular for a minute."

Rowen got up as close as he could without going on the grass. He handed her the monocular. "What does it say, Purdy?"

Purdy knelt down and adjusted the spy tool to read the medal. "It says, 'St. Christopher Protect Us' on the front, and the lettering on the back says, *To Sophie from Mom!*'"

"Hurray! Now we have a clue about the other girl," said Rowen. "We just need to find out who Sophie is." Purdy nodded in agreement.

They turned to head toward home. Rowen tapped Purdy on the arm and spoke to her, along with his limited sign language. She watched him patiently.

"It's important to know that a St. Christopher's medal is for protection. This medallion tells us something about the girl who lost it. For one, she comes from a religious family, and two, someone cares about her and wants her to be protected. So, Sophie isn't all bad."

Purdy said, "I wonder what would make her send those awful notes?"

Chapter 10
Telling Rowen

Dog

I t had been a week since Purdy's tenth birthday. She still hadn't told Rowen that she became a cat every night at 10:00 p.m. and turned back into a girl the next morning.

Rowen was her best friend, and Purdy needed to tell him. She decided to go out on Friday night and show up at Rowen's house as a cat. She carefully prepared before cat time. First, Purdy left her bedroom door ajar, like she had before. She removed Beau's collar from around his neck and wrote a note:

Rowen, It's Me, Persephone. I become a cat at night.

Purdy folded the note tightly and taped it around her cat's collar.

She placed the collar around her own neck as tightly as possible before sleeping. It was only 7:00 p.m., but she was still tired from the night before. Once she woke up as a cat, Purdy was ready to tell her secret to Rowen.

The collar fit loosely around *her* cat-neck, and she hoped it wouldn't fall off when she went out for the night.

Purdy peeked her head through the open bedroom door and looked around. The way was clear, so she walked cautiously before realizing that one of her sisters was leaving her own bedroom. Kara spotted Purdy, and before she could leap down the stairs and leave the house, her sister scooped her up and held her tightly!

"I knew it," said Kara.

Her sister's words were like a rush of wind blowing in Purdy's face, but at least she was close enough to read her lips.

"I knew Persephone was hiding a stray cat in her room." She then took out her phone and snapped a picture of Purdy. "I just took a picture of you, so now I have proof! I have a picture, and pictures don't lie."

Oh dear, now my sister has a picture of me as a cat. I wonder what she plans to do with that! Wait! That's the same message The Unkindness Club *used in some of their notes. 'I have pictures, and pictures don't lie!' Could my sister Kara be the one behind the notes?*

Purdy squirmed and howled deep in her throat. When she turned around in Kara's arms, her sister could no longer hold onto her. It was as if Purdy had no bones and became a slinky, wiggly toy, without much stuffing.

Purdy got away and was halfway down the stairs before Kara could do anything about it.

She was glad she didn't have to scratch or bite her sister to get away. She leaped down the rest of the steps, streaked through the kitchen, and left the house through the cat door flap leading to the backyard. She stopped there and made sure she was still wearing Beau's collar. It was there, luckily. *It's a good thing Kara didn't take off the collar and see my note.*

She ran around to the front of her home. Night had descended, and the temperature was falling. Leaves twirled in the wind. This September night seemed colder than the night before. Purdy could see her breath in front of her little cat body, and frost droplets formed on her whiskers.

She had learned to take shortcuts by following Beau. But this time was different because she was alone in the dark. The words 'scaredy cat' came to mind. She saw glowing eyes watching her from every direction. It was good that she couldn't hear the night sounds around her, without her hearing aids, as she made her way toward Rowen's home. Walking on all fours was still a new adventure, with her head so close to the ground. She noticed things in this new position, like lines on the sidewalk and the length of the grass, that humans didn't notice when they were upright at about four feet tall.

Purdy arrived at Rowen's house. She knew he usually stayed up late on his computer when he didn't have school the next day.

Purdy checked for a light in his main-floor bedroom window, just in case. The light was still on. She ran along the walkway and leaped up the few front steps to his gray house with the wide white porch and purple door, where she had entered many times over the years. The house now seemed huge to a little cat. She let out a shiver, not just from the cold autumn air, but because everything looked bigger and spookier to her in the dark of night.

Purdy had no idea how loud she meowed. She couldn't hear a sound, but she could feel herself vibrate. Purdy tried her cat voice a few times at different degrees of intensity with no reaction. She decided to give it all she had. It could have been a roar, a screech, or a howl that came out of her mouth; she wasn't sure.

That time, it worked, and she got a reaction. The front porch light came on, and Purdy saw the door crack open. Purdy looked up into Rowen's mother's face. "Who is it?" She looked around, shook her head, and began to close the door.

Thinking fast, Purdy let out a much quieter sound. Suddenly, the door flew open, and not only was his mother there, but she also saw Rowen.

"Mom. Mom, it's only a cat," said Rowen. He wheeled his chair through the door and onto the porch. Purdy jumped onto his lap. By the look on his face, she could tell that this startled him.

"I think it likes you," said his mother. "You'd better check to see if there's a name or phone number on the collar."

Rowen noticed the collar tag. He read the name of Purdy's cat, Beau, with Purdy's phone number on it. "But wait. What's this?" Rowen grabbed the folded paper from the cat's collar, unfolded it, and read Purdy's note.

Rowen, It's Me, Persephone. I become a cat every night.

Rowen gasped, nearly dropping the note.

"What is it?" asked his mom.

Downplaying the serious situation, Rowen said, "It's nothing, Mom. The collar says the name of Persephone's cat, Beau, and has her phone number. I'll let this cat warm up before sending it home."

Rowen allowed Purdy to stay on his lap as he wheeled his chair through the front door, along a wheelchair-friendly wooden floor, and opened the door to his room, which also had a doorknob set low enough so he could reach it. He then wheeled himself and Purdy into his first-floor bedroom.

When the door was closed, he held Purdy close to his face and said, "Hey Purdy, is that you?'

She read his lips and meowed.

"Purdy, I thought you said it was only a dream. Do you really turn into a cat? I just saw you at school, and you weren't a cat then. I noticed your note saying you turn into a cat at night."

He grabbed a bell from his parakeet's cage, which hung low enough for him to reach from his chair. "If it's you, then ring this bell."

Purdy licked her lips at the thought of eating Rowen's bird. She pictured yellow feathers flying as she jumped high enough to catch a flying bird. Although that seemed more interesting than ringing the bell, she had to shake herself and try to smother thoughts of eating Rowen's pet.

Purdy got onto her hind legs and batted at the small bell, which hung from a string in Rowen's hand. He said, "Well, I think cats just naturally like to ring bells, so that doesn't prove anything." Rowen returned the bell and closed the cage tightly.

Rowen looked thoughtful for a minute before pointing at a digital piano on the other side of the room. "Purdy, if that's you, then play something on my piano."

What? Rowen, don't you know how hard that is for a cat? I'll have to play a song without thumbs and fingers. She paced the floor, circling his chair a few times, hoping he would change his mind. He pointed at the keyboard again. She read his lips when he said, "If it's you, then I know you can play the piano, so show me!"

Okay, Rowen, you're always so stubborn. I'll show you who's a cat! With her nose in the air and her tail held high, Purdy sauntered to the digital keyboard and jumped up. She pawed at each note, playing *Twinkle, Twinkle Little Star.*

Rowen wheeled himself over to where Purdy had just finished playing her song, grabbed her, and twirled her around so he could look her in the eye.

"Purdy! You *are* a cat! It's incredible! How? Why? I wonder how this is possible. It's a scientific wonder! It's a freak of nature! An amazing breakthrough!" His face turned so red that his freckles seemed to glow on his face. "Purdy, just think of all the amazing places you can go. With you as a cat, we can solve mysteries and crimes together. The possibilities are endless!" Rowen made the hand signs of firecrackers going off. "Whoa, this blows me away. My mom didn't even suspect that she was letting *you* into her home. This proves that an innocent little cat could go anywhere!"

He held her up once more, so she could read his lips. "I know you can't talk, and I'm pretty sure you can't hear me."

He set her on his lap and wheeled his chair through the kitchen. "Purdy, I'll let you out the back door, and we can talk tomorrow. I can't wait to hear what this is like for you." The door handle was low enough for Rowen to open it on his own. Purdy jumped down from his chair and ran outside.

Chapter 11
A Small Cat in a Big World

Cat

P urdy was outside in Rowen's backyard. Because of her improved night vision, she could see the figure of a dog, with its teeth bared, coming toward her. The dog's mouth was moving, and the movements and vibrations she felt indicated to Purdy that he was barking.

Purdy knew Rowen had two black labradors, but she could only see one dog now. She always liked his dogs; they never bothered her before, but this dog seemed threatening to a small cat.

What should she do? She was no match for a dog. As a girl, a dog that size, who knew her scent wouldn't have been a problem, but as a cat, she felt helpless.

For the second time, Purdy felt like her heart would beat right out of her chest. The first time was on the night she first became a cat.

Her hackles came up, her tail flared, and her back arched. *This must be how artists got the idea of a scary Halloween cat.*

Purdy spotted an opening under Rowen's back porch where she could hide. She peeked through the backside of the wooden slats. She felt the ground shake from the pacing dog near the space where she was hiding. The pacing went on for so long that she didn't dare come out and try to get away. Purdy had never tried out her short cat legs at a fast pace, so she was uncertain whether she could outrun Rowen's dog.

Feeling exhausted from this ordeal, yet trying to wait out the dog, Purdy felt her eyelids getting heavy. Much like the first night when Purdy became a cat, she curled up under Rowen's porch and went to sleep. She gave no thought to the consequences.

Purdy woke up with the sun streaming through wooden slats. *Where am I, and how did I get here?*

She peeked out and saw frosty grass, fallen leaves, and a pathway to a doghouse. A shiver ran through her. She was cold without the comforting cat fur that had covered her moments before.

A doghouse! Oh no! She remembered hiding under Rowen's back porch and waiting for his dog to stop pacing. *I must have fallen asleep. Now what?* Cats don't need to wear clothes, but girls do. Purdy was now a girl in an embarrassing situation, with no easy way out!

The clothesline held crisp clothing lined up and pinned in neat rows. The wind blew, causing T-shirts and dresses to billow like kites in the breeze.

The dog was no longer in sight, so it was now safe for her to leave. But how could she leave without a way to cover up? *I need something I can wrap up in long enough to get home.* She noticed a blue floral blanket that had blown off the clothesline and landed within a few feet of the porch.

Purdy inched out of the small opening and stretched out her human arm, crawling her fingers along the grass until she felt the soft fabric of the blanket. She then tugged it inside her hiding hole and wrapped herself up like one of her mama's burritos. The blanket felt cold against her skin at first, but soon it warmed and comforted her. She then crawled out from under the porch and looked around.

Purdy hoped one of Rowen's dogs wouldn't alert the household that she was there. She also hoped it was early enough, on a Saturday, so that no one would be nearby. There could be some folks around early on a Saturday. For instance, what about a paperboy? Or the mailman.

Trying to make herself seem small and looking shifty-eyed around her, Purdy made her way to the sidewalk. She never thought she would wish to be a cat, but at that moment, being a cat would have been much more practical.

Purdy covered her hair with the flowered blanket because her white-streaked, black hair—and emerald, green eyes, for that matter, would be a giveaway. And people would immediately know that it was Persephone.

Chapter 12
Getting Caught

Caught

Before she had gone far, a black convertible with the top closed pulled close to her, moving slowly. Purdy recognized the car and knew right away it was her grandmother's. In her mind, she was saying over and over—*please keep going. Please, please, please don't stop!* But the car stopped. *At least Grandma didn't honk her horn.*

She had been hoping to slither away unnoticed, but now this! How could all of this happen to her? And why? Now, she would have to think up an excuse to tell her grandma.

Grandma parked her car, opened the door, and motioned for Purdy to climb in.

Grandma will wonder why I'm out so early in the morning, wearing only a blanket. What should I tell her? How can I explain where I spent the night? Why would a ten-year-old girl spend the night under a boy's porch?

Purdy hesitated to get into the car. She couldn't think of any logical reason for her to be in that situation.

I won't explain that I went out as a cat, and now I'm a girl. Or that I had to grab a blanket to cover myself up. Gulp!

Holding tightly to the blanket with only her face visible, Purdy joined her grandma in the car and squeaked, "I don't have my hearing aids in, Grandma."

Her grandmother looked as though she hadn't slept much, with her messy salt and pepper hair falling into her face and her clothes rumpled. She spoke using words and sign language, as Purdy's family often did.

Grandma said, "Persephone, dear, you do not need to explain a thing to me."

With wide eyes, Purdy uncovered her head from under the blanket, "What do you mean, Grandma?"

Facing Purdy and still signing, Grandma said, "I know what is going on here, and you don't need to worry. Your secret is safe with me. For now."

"My secret, Grandma? Do you already know my secret? But how?"

Grandma continued to speak and sign. "Yes, I do. And you don't need to explain what happened to you because it also happens to me. I, too, turn into a cat."

Purdy gulped in a huge amount of air and held her breath too long before speaking. "A cat? You are also a cat?"

Grandma nodded curtly, "Indeed, I am. I am now an old calico cat." Grandma made eyeglass shapes with her fingers over her eyes. "Without my glasses, my vision is not so good." She then put both hands behind her ears. "But my hearing is very sharp."

Purdy gulped again. *How can this be?* "Oh, Grandma, I can't *hear*, but my eyesight is good—especially when I'm a cat!"

Once again, her grandmother nodded. She wrapped her arms in front of her and rubbed them with her hands. "It's cold out here!" She then made the motions of driving. "I will drive you home and ring the doorbell while you go in through the back door,"

Purdy shivered. But this time, it was from relief that her grandmother understood the situation she was in.

Chapter 13
Eavesdropping

Purdy left the car, still holding tight to the floral blanket that was the only thing covering her. She ran and tripped over the blanket twice before reaching the back door. She noticed her mother through the window, with her black hair pulled away from her face. When the front doorbell rang, her mother wiped her hands on her apron and left the kitchen. Purdy let herself in through the back door and quietly went toward the front staircase. She reached the stairs and saw her mother talking to her grandmother in the doorway. Once again, Purdy tripped on the blanket and fell up the steps.

Grandma tried to distract her mama, but it didn't work. Her mother turned around and saw her daughter going up the stairs with the blue blanket tucked closely around her.

Purdy glanced back and saw her mama's dark eyes, so large that they might fall out, and her hands flung into the air. In one hand, her mother held a light-green envelope, which she had no doubt removed from the door.

Her grandmother entered the house and motioned for Purdy to continue up the steps. She put her arm around Purdy's mother and guided her toward the kitchen.

As Purdy continued up the steps, her cat, Beau, ran past her and streaked down the stairs. She approached her bedroom, opened the door, and flopped onto her bed. Purdy was tired but wanted to hear what her grandmother said to her mother. Purdy discarded the blanket on the floor in the corner of her room. She dressed into her PJs, placed her hearing aids in both ears, and then brushed her hair to remove any sticks and leaves left over from her night under the porch.

Purdy grabbed her small voice recorder and entered the kitchen as if she had just woken up on an ordinary Saturday morning. But this wasn't a regular day.

Purdy flipped on the recorder before grabbing a bowl from the cupboard, taking out a box of cereal, and then grabbing a gallon of milk from the fridge. The two women kept talking. Occasionally, a voice would rise, and her mother would exclaim something in Spanish.

Purdy faked disinterest in the conversation, all the while making a recording, so she could listen to it later.

Something else was going on in the breakfast nook. Purdy parked herself in front of the TV to watch Saturday morning cartoons. The TV had a router that streamed sound directly into her hearing aids, but she didn't turn up the sound.

With her recorder in hand, Purdy stayed just out of sight and crept closer to the door where her twin sisters sat talking. She was close enough to read their lips, but they had their hands to the side of their mouths, as if they were telling secrets. Purdy didn't know what her sisters were saying. When their conversation ended, she clicked off the recorder, turned off the TV, put her bowl in the sink, and headed back upstairs so she could listen to the recordings.

Hooking her recorder to Bluetooth, she listened to the conversation, streaming directly into her hearing aids.

Purdy recorded this:

"Kara, did you read your note?"

"Yes, sister. I read my note. Who could know that I'm always running late for school? The note said someone saw me get onto the bus and exit without paying. It also said, 'I have pictures and pictures don't lie.'"

Tara said, "Oh wow. Mine says that the Unkindness Club has pictures of me kissing another girl's boyfriend. Really? Whose boyfriend was I kissing? The pictures show me kissing my boyfriend, Kevin. So, if he has another girlfriend, that's his fault, not mine! And ewe! I don't want to date a two-timer, so I will ask lots of questions."

Kara asked, "Who do you think sent it?"

Tara answered, "I don't know!"

Tara switched topics and said, "Hey, Persephone has a new cat that sneaks in and out of the house at night. I've seen the black and white cat coming through her bedroom door."

"I know," said Kara. "I caught that cat the other day, but it slithered right out of my grasp and slinked down the steps. I haven't seen it since."

Tara said, "I have a plan to catch that cat. I'll start putting cat treats outside our bedroom door, and when it comes to eat them, I'll grab the cat and keep it in our room."

"Do you think that'll work?" asked Kara.

Tara giggled. "You'll see, cats can't resist those treats. And I've already made a tag for *my* cat, with the name Rosie and my phone number. That cat will soon be mine!"

So, they are up to something! thought Purdy.

Purdy finally got up the courage to listen to her grandma explain her transformation to her mother.

Grandma said, "Malina, you just saw your daughter trying her best to deal with her gift."

Mama said, "Mother, you aren't making any sense."

Grandma said, "Yes, Malina. Persephone has a gift, just like me."

Mama asked, "Like you, Mother? Are you trying to say that Persephone is. . . is?"

Grandma said, "Yes, dear. Persephone is a cat, just like me."

Mama said, "My daughter, a cat? Did she get the gift that skipped a generation? When? How did this happen, Mother?"

Grandma said, "I have no idea how she hid it from us, but of course, it happened on her tenth birthday, just like it did with me. I wondered if the gift was gone from this family altogether. But it's still here, alive and well."

Mama said, "Oh wow! That is such a surprise and a relief. I wondered why Persephone got up early and went to bed before ten. So, that's it then?"

Grandma said, "That's it. I need to teach your daughter how to use her gift and what to do if she wakes up in a strange place with..."

Mama said, "Without her clothes? Oh dear, Mother, do you think that's what happened today?"

Grandma said, "I know it did, dear. Persephone became a cat last night and woke up under her best friend's porch. She was lucky to find a blanket and didn't have to roll in the mud. It's a very good thing that I was there this morning."

"Well done, Mother! You need to train her. It's obvious that this is not going away. If you insist this is a gift and not a curse, I will allow you to handle it."

Chapter 14
Mama Knows

Now, not only did Purdy's grandmother know her secret, but her mama also knew.

I guess Grandma couldn't really keep my secret, once Mama saw me sneaking into the house, covered by a blanket.

Later that day, her mother took her aside and asked, "Persephone, can I do anything to help you? I know what you're going through now, after talking to your grandma. I remember waking up at night as a child and finding a cat sleeping in the bed where my mama should have been. Instead of looking for my mama, I would curl up with the little cat, which always made me feel better. Other times, when I had a bad dream, the cat would come into my bed and sleep with me. I didn't know until I got older that the cat *was* my mama.

"How can I help you now, honey?" asked Mama.

Purdy held her head down and answered shyly, "Mama, there are a few things I need. I need to have a cat door put into my bedroom door." Lifting her head, Purdy smirked and said, "You know so that Beau can get in and out of my room."

Her mama winked, knowing what she meant. "Sure, sure," said Mama. "Anything else?"

"I need to have a key to keep in a safe place outside in case I get locked out of the house."

Feeling more confident now, Purdy said, "Mama, I followed my cat Beau the other night, and he led me to a mother cat and her little kittens. At first, I thought they were *his* kittens, but then I remembered that he was a house cat and had an operation. They couldn't be his."

Her mama nodded.

"Mama, could we adopt a few of those kittens, I mean, after they're big enough to be taken from their mother?" asked Purdy.

"Well, yes," said Mama. "I think we could. But how many are there?"

"There are six."

"We can't keep all six, but we could bring them here, along with the mother cat, until they are big enough to give away. That is, only if the mother cat allows it. And then we could keep one or two and find homes for the rest," said Mama.

Purdy's dad wasn't told that she was a *cat* when she found the kittens. He only knew that she had seen her cat, Beau, go into the garage.

On Sunday, Purdy's dad agreed to help her rescue the mama cat and her babies. Purdy fitted a cardboard box with a small pillow to make it comfortable for the cat and her babies. They got into her dad's truck, and she described where she had last seen the kittens. They picked up Rowen from his house, put his manual wheelchair in the back of the truck, and drove to the old garage where the new mother cat kept her kittens. Rowen waited in the truck for Purdy and her dad to return.

"Over here, Dad!" said Purdy. Although the sun shone brightly on the fall day, it seemed dark and shadowy around the garage from overgrown trees and shrubs. Her dad looked in through a broken window on the side of the building.

"I don't see any cats. This place seems dirty and filled with discarded junk," said her dad.

"Oh, they're in there. I'll show you," said Purdy.

"What's the best way to get in?" asked her dad.

"I'll try the door first; if that doesn't work, you could break out the rest of the glass and hoist me in through the window," said Purdy.

Although the knob was loose and wobbly, the side door opened easily with a creak.

Carrying the prepared box, Purdy headed straight to the corner where she had seen the cat family.

The mother cat must have recognized Purdy's scent and didn't seem alarmed when she carefully picked up each kitten by its scruff and placed them, one by one, into the box. Purdy licked her lips, remembering when she carried a tiny kitten in her own mouth.

The mother cat sniffed the box, then climbed in and joined her little family. Purdy's dad carried them to his truck, with Purdy following close behind, speaking softly to her new cat friends.

When they reached the truck, Rowen asked, "Purdy, did you find the kittens?"

"Yes, they're all here, safe and sound," she answered. She held the box up so Rowen could see inside.

"Oh wow! They are so tiny. What will you do now?" he asked.

Before driving away, her dad faced Purdy from the driver's seat and answered, "Persephone has everything figured out. She set up a litter box in our garage. She also has small bowls, some with cat food and others with either kitten food or water." He winked at Purdy. "The baby nursery is ready."

When they pulled into the driveway, her father opened the garage door; he took out Rowen's wheelchair and unfolded it. Rowen needed help getting out of the high truck and into his wheelchair.

Rowen offered to carry the box, so Purdy gently lifted the cat box from the back of the truck and placed it on Rowen's lap. She then wheeled him into the garage with the kittens, eyes now open, mewing softly and walking around inside the box.

"I'm going to name the mother cat Sassy," said Purdy.

Her dad watched while Purdy gently placed the box next to the litter box, food, and water bowls. She then backed up slowly, and Rowen retreated in his chair.

Her dad went through to the backyard and said he would keep an eye on the cats.

The two kids entered the house through the kitchen door, which had no steps.

When Purdy and Rowen checked on them later, the mother cat was carrying one of the kittens by its scruff and going out the cat door from the garage.

Purdy motioned for Rowen, "Check the cat box. How many kittens are in there?"

"Only one, Purdy!"

"Oh dear. I'll follow Sassy to see where she's taking her babies."

Purdy slowly followed the cat. The mother had placed her babies in a large, empty flowerpot behind a trash can.

She ran to get her dad. "Dad, Sassy is moving her kittens. What should we do?"

"Go get the box, Honey. I guess she's not comfortable being inside the garage."

"Well, she *was* in a garage before, Dad."

"That's true. I have no idea what spooked her. Let me put the box inside the old playhouse. That way, she'll still be outside but have a shelter as she did in the old garage. That way, we can keep an eye on them and still feed them."

Purdy handed Rowen the box with one remaining kitten inside. He carried the box in his chair along the cement pathways of the backyard.

Purdy and her dad gathered the remaining kittens and returned them to the box. Then Purdy's dad placed the box in the playhouse. This time, Sassy returned to the box and stayed with her babies.

Purdy moved the small bowls near the cat's box.

Purdy and Rowen watched to ensure the mother and her family were safe. Beau also paced back and forth, watching over his cat family.

As they sat in the backyard, keeping an eye on the mother cat and her kittens, Rowen pulled out his phone to check the laws for pet licensing. "Purdy, only three pets are allowed in a home in Salt Lake County. A family can ask for permission to keep a fourth pet."

"Let's see. We now have two adult cats and six kittens. That's a total of eight cats," said Purdy.

"Wait a minute, Purdy. If we count you, when you're a cat, that makes nine!" said Rowen.

"Oh yeah, you're right, but I don't think animal control would come at night," said Purdy.

Rowen continued to read, "A pet needs to be licensed when they turn four months old."

"Beau is licensed, the mama cat isn't licensed, but the kittens are still too young," said Purdy. "And then, there is me, of course."

Chapter 15
Purdy's Note

Purdy received her own note the next day, in a violet envelope, taped to their front door. Purdy took down the note and read aloud.

Persephone Franklin,

It has been brought to my attention that you have more than the legal limit of pets in your household. I have counted three adult cats and six kittens on your property. Only one cat is licensed. I have proof, and pictures don't lie. If you don't handle this problem immediately, I will report you to animal control.

A Concerned Citizen

Three pictures fell out of the envelope. One was Purdy, as a black and white cat—if she wasn't mistaken, it could be the picture her sister Kara took a few nights ago (which could mean her sister sent the note). One was her marmalade cat, Beau, and the other was the mama cat with her six kittens in the backyard playhouse. If her sister hadn't taken the pictures, then not only was someone watching, but they must have been trespassing on the Franklins' property.

Purdy read the note over and over. Unlike The Unkindness Club notes she'd seen at school and the one that fell on the ground a few nights before, this note was signed *A Concerned Citizen.*

Who wrote this note? Why would they care that we had a cat with a box of kittens living outside our house?

She was suspicious of her sisters, even though they received their own notes. Why would Kara take her picture as a cat and then say, "I have a picture, and pictures don't lie?" The Unkindness Club made the same statement in so many other notes received by kids at school. After recording her sisters in the breakfast nook, Purdy knew that it bothered them that she had a new cat, and that was even before she brought home a mother cat with six kittens. If her sisters weren't involved, then maybe Kara told her friend Elenore about the kittens offhandedly.

Purdy searched online to see what she could do about getting a pet license. A license in her county would require an online application, a fee, plus proof of vaccinations and sterilization.

Vaccinations are impossible for me. I can't see a vet for vaccinations and sterilization. No way. For one thing, I'm only a cat at night. Eeow! She shuddered; *things keep getting worse.*

Purdy showed the note to her mama, who was also alarmed. "This means that someone has been snooping around our property! Someone took a picture of you as a cat, which could only happen at night, and now this note. Who would do that and why?"

"I don't know, Mama. The only other person I talked to about the cat and her kittens was Rowen."

A few days later, she received a second note on plain white paper, taped to the front door. This note had different handwriting and there was no mention of The Unkindness Club or A Concerned Citizen. This time, Purdy was certain the note was from her best friend, Rowen. The note said:

P, I have a solution for your unlicensed pet problem. Meet me at the park tonight at 11:00 p.m. and bring your cat.

R

Chapter 16
A Trap?

Purdy was eager to get the problem behind her. She knew from the Unkindness Club note she received before that someone was watching her house. She had too many cats on her property and was excited to hear Rowen's solution. Purdy could hardly wait to meet him in the park, as a cat that night.

After turning into a cat that night at 10:00 pm. Purdy left her room through the new cat door. She looked up and down the hallway to be sure the coast was clear, then stealthily ran down the stairs and left the house through the kitchen.

It seemed creepy for Rowen to meet her at the park after dark.

At around 11:00 p.m. (Purdy couldn't really tell time as a cat), she leaped onto a park bench and walked back and forth. Besides the limited light from the streetlights, everything was dark, which caused long shadows.

Purdy grew anxious while waiting for Rowen, and scary thoughts began to creep in.

If Rowen wants to see me as a cat, he only needs to ask. I don't need to meet him in a park to talk. Wait, the note didn't say to come as a cat. It told me to bring my cat!

Ah! This note wasn't from Rowen! Whoever wrote it didn't know that I would come as a cat. The note was a trap! I need to leave now!

Purdy leaped over the back of the bench and started for the bushes.

Just then, she saw a large man coming up behind her. Purdy was sure he was speaking to her, but no words got through to her. She tried to run, but it didn't seem like her small paws were going anywhere. He advanced toward her with a large net. The net, attached to a long pole, came down and caught her. Purdy, the small black and white cat, was trapped!

Purdy noticed two figures dressed in dark clothing standing near the bench where she had been moments before. *Those are probably the same two people who delivered the unkindness notes!*

Chapter 17
Wish It Were Rowen!

Purdy struggled to get away, but it was no use. Someone had set a trap for her, and she fell right into it.

Purdy wanted to ask, *Who told you I was unlicensed and that I would be here?* But she was a cat and unable to speak. The animal catcher put her into a cage in the back of a pet rescue truck. The two dark figures advanced toward the truck and peered in through a small window. They were gesturing, and their shoulders shook. She was sure the two people were laughing, but she couldn't make out their faces.

Other caged animals surrounded Purdy.

When the truck arrived at the pet rescue, the rescue officer removed Purdy from the truck and took her inside a large room, where he transferred her to a slightly larger cage with a water bowl and a handful of kibbles.

There was no way to reach Rowen, her mom, or her grandmother. No one would know where she was. The enclosure had a grid of thin metal wires. The cage door was closed by a small metal bar through a loop on the outside. It would be difficult for a small cat to escape the cage on its own. There was no way out. All night long, she sensed the helplessness of the other caged animals. Thankfully, she couldn't hear their desperate cries.

A pile of old clothes for use as a temporary pet bed lay in the corner of her cage. The clothes smelled clean. Purdy curled up and tried to sleep. She still hoped Rowen had sent her the note, letting her know he had a solution to her pet problem. If it were Rowen, at least he would have seen her show up at the park, and he'd know where she was now.

Purdy Franklin—caged animal. What will they do to me now? Will they chip me, spay me, and inject me with feline vaccines? At least cats have nine lives. But I have already lived two lives: One as a girl with a family who mostly loved me—but I'm not always sure how my sisters feel about me at times—and now I'm living the life of a kidnapped pet.

What will happen to me? Will an injection change me into a cat forever?

If I become a cat forever, will I still understand humans? Will my grandmother, as a cat, be able to find me and communicate with me in cat language?

Will the person who wrote that note ever figure out what harm they have caused me?

It was cold and dark in the room with multiple animal cages. The only lights came from a few nightlights and an Exit sign. Purdy snuggled into the pile of clothes. She didn't care whose clothes they were. They felt soft and comfy.

She tried to sleep, but her thoughts continued: Will *someone try to adopt me? No!* She ruled that out. She wouldn't be adopted before morning, and she'd no longer be a cat in the morning—she would turn back into a girl.

Chapter 18
A Big Girl in a Small Cage

Purdy must have fallen asleep sometime during the night. She woke to morning light streaming in through high, barred windows. Once again, she woke up in a strange place, as a girl without her clothes.

I'm sure this isn't a dream. After being picked up as a cat last night, I've turned back into a girl, in a cage made for a cat.

The cage was wider than it was deep and anything but comfortable. Without moving much, she knocked over the food and water bowls. Hunched over, Purdy did her best to sort through the clothing left in her cage. She found a large, brown men's work shirt in the pile, a stretchy pair of red tights, a pink tutu, and a boy's blue plaid cowboy shirt.

These clothes seemed comfortable when I was sleeping last night. Now, what can I wear to get myself out of here?

Purdy wished she could look through the clothing in one of the other animal cages, but that wouldn't be possible.

These clothes are wet and wrinkled, but they still smell clean. Purdy put on the tights, the tutu, and the cowboy shirt, leaving the man's shirt on the cage floor. *This shirt might soak up the rest of the water.* The colors didn't match, and neither did the style.

I know my day will be much better than my thoughts and fears from last night. I will soon be free! And I'll get to the bottom of this!

Purdy tried to reach through the metal grid to the rod and loop that locked her cage from the outside. But if this was too small for a tiny cat to reach through, how could a ten-year-old's hand open it from the inside? Her cage was about waist-high from the ground and must have been seated on a ledge. She rocked the cage back and forth, hoping it would come loose from the shelf, but it didn't move much. Besides, she was sure she would get hurt if the cage fell.

Purdy decided to yell out. "Get me out of here!" There was no human response. Her yelling started the dogs near her running in their cages, and their voices vibrated around her.

Purdy sat with her knees up to her chest, but her back couldn't straighten up. She sat like that, rocking back and forth. With her eyes closed, she mouthed the words and signed the song, "The Cat Came Back." The cat came back the very next day. She thought she was a goner, but the cat came back!"

Purdy's eyes flew open when she sensed someone nearby. The morning workers were busy opening cages and refreshing the water and food bowls.

It took two people to feed each animal. She noticed that one was a standby person to make sure the animals didn't bite someone or get loose.

When she saw them near, she began yelling and banging on the side of her cage with the empty water bowl. "Get me out of here! How dare you kidnap me this way! If I needed a cage, you could at least give me one of a decent size! Get me out of here, now!" She wasn't sure how loud she was yelling because she didn't have her hearing aids.

The two workers ran toward the cage where Purdy was trapped.

Their hands flew into the air, and their faces looked shocked. They were so surprised that they didn't let her out. Instead, they took off running down the hall and through a door. They must have been yelling something, but Purdy wasn't sure.

"But what about me? You guys can't just leave me here! It's mean to keep me in a cage. Please get me out. Get me out of here!"

Purdy didn't want anyone to know she was a cat, but how would someone explain that a girl got into a cage locked from the outside?

Chapter 19
One Phone Call

Phone / Call

The two workers returned with two men in uniforms. Purdy began to yell again. "I don't belong here! I'm a girl, not a pet. You can't just leave me in this cage!"

Keys dangled from the belt of the man in charge. When he saw Purdy, he wore a look of terror. He said something to Purdy, but she couldn't hear him. He held up a finger and snapped several pictures of Purdy seated hunched over in the small cage. She wasn't smiling.

He then moved a short ladder against her cage and unlocked her prison. He gently helped Purdy out of the enclosure and helped her walk toward the front with his mouth moving, his head shaking, and his hands moving frantically. Although she couldn't hear him, Purdy assumed he was apologizing.

When they reached his desk, she noticed a plaque with the name Officer Robert Manns.

Turning the speaker on, he handed her the receiver for the desk phone and let her make a call. Before making the call, Purdy told Robert Manns, "I'm calling my grandma, Mrs. Cruz. I'm sure she will come and pick me up."

"Grandma, it's Persephone. Can you come and get me? I'm
at the animal shelter."

Purdy handed the phone back to Mr. Manns. "I'm deaf," she said, pointing to her ears. Will you talk to my grandma for me, please?"

Once again, his mouth moved. She read his lips when he said, "You poor girl, alone and scared." He took the receiver from Purdy and spoke to her grandmother.

Purdy picked up the phone again,

"Grandma, I don't have my hearing aids. I was picked up in
the park last night. Someone reported me as an unlicensed
pet, but I don't know who. I saw two people in black hoods
again. I spent the night in a cage. I'm dirty, hungry and tired.
There are a lot of scared pets here. I had a hard time sleeping.
I want to go home, Grandma. Please!"

Purdy handed the phone back to Robert. She looked around at the workers, all watching her curiously.

When her grandmother arrived, the manager and another man walked Purdy out to the car.   Grandma signed words to Purdy, telling her to wait in the car. While sitting in the car, Purdy watched the workers' expressions as they spoke with Grandma. She watched Grandma gesture with her hands and decided she must have been speaking about the cage she spent the night in.   Purdy noticed sad expressions on the men's faces.

She positioned herself so she could read their lips, but she could only grasp a few words while the conversation moved back and forth, and a speaker turned away for a moment or put a hand in front of their faces.   A man was saying, "Ma'am, – ---- child okay? – ---- no idea — — got trapped -----. – ----- something we can --? You're not ----- – press charges, — you? I mean, no one ------ ------------ cage a child."

Purdy assumed her grandma knew she was watching the conversation. Grandma spoke slowly and signed the words as she spoke. "My granddaughter loves animals, and she is a curious one. But you do realize that someone locked the cage from the outside?"

Grandma continued. "Who reported an animal in the park where animal control picked her up? Who picked her up and put her in the cage? I'll need a full report. Do you understand? I will go to the press if I don't have all the information."

Mr. Manns excitedly waved his hands and pointed to himself. "Yes, -----. I'll get it; you will have the info ------. I'll make this -----. — ----- this right, ma'am. That poor girl. – ---- have been so frightening – – ------ up that way. — — who --------- an unlicensed cat – --------- at fault here. You will have this ----------- before — end – — week.

With the words she did manage to read on their lips, she began to put the pieces of a puzzle together in her mind.

Grandma got into the car. While sitting in the parking lot, Purdy told her grandmother about the note she had received, which said she had too many pets. "I only spoke to Rowen and my mom about the first note."

Grandma signed to Purdy, "So, there was a second note?"

Purdy answered, "Yes, but the second note was in different handwriting. It said there was a solution to my pet problem, and I should come to the park at 11:00 p.m. and bring my cat. The note writer signed an R. I thought it was from Rowen."

Purdy continued, "Grandma, I was so worried. I thought I would be spayed and given injections, and I was afraid I might never be a girl again."

Grandma clicked her tongue and shook her head in sympathy "Persephone, you must not, under any circumstances, be spayed or given an injection that might change you. I don't know for sure, but you could become a cat permanently. This note wasn't just a warning; it was a threat! Whoever did this to you may know that you're a cat, and they may be trying to mess things up for you. We need to find them and fix this. And soon!"

Purdy said, "I know, Grandma, but I don't think the note sender knows I'm a cat because their note told me to *bring my cat*. Could my sisters be doing this? I recorded one of their conversation last week. They complained that a new cat was coming in and out of my room and wanted to catch the cat I become. That was before I brought the mama cat and her six kittens home. Do you think my sisters sent the note yesterday? Could they be part of The Unkindness Club?"

Grandma said, "I, I don't think your sisters would do that. Besides, they got unkindness notes as well. I didn't read them, but. . ."

Chapter 20
Following the Clues

I wonder if Grandma has any more information from animal control. They don't want the public to know about a ten-year-old girl spending the night in a cat cage! But if we push it too much, someone might discover that I was picked up as a cat and then turned back into a girl!

The next day, Grandma received a phone call from animal control. She put the phone on speaker and recorded the call so Purdy could listen later.

"Mrs. Cruz, this is Animal Control Officer Robert Manns. Do you have a minute?"

"Yes, yes," said Grandma.

"We have the information you requested."

"Yes," said Grandma curiously.

"The call about an unlicensed animal came in at 7:00 p.m., and the call came from an unlisted number. The caller was a woman who stated there was an unlicensed cat—a small black-and-white cat without a license. The caller also mentioned a dark-haired, deaf girl who owned the cat and would be at the park around 11:00 pm last night. Our information was that our officer could find the cat around a park bench near the pavilion. The only other information was that the cat was a nuisance, making loud screeching sounds and going through trash cans, which made a mess in the neighborhood, especially at night."

Mr. Manns continued,

"The caller told me, 'If you could catch this cat, it would be helpful to the neighborhood.' Then the caller thanked me repeatedly, saying she would be waiting nearby. I told the reporting party, 'I need your name, Ma'am. Who will I say is reporting this?' The woman said, 'Let's just say I'm a concerned citizen,' and she hung up."

"Thank you for sharing this information," said Grandma.

Grandma ended the call and turned to Purdy.

"Persephone, I'm going to play back the recording so you can hear my conversation with the Animal Control officer."

Purdy connected the Bluetooth to her hearing aid and listened to the whole conversation. After listening to the recorded call, Purdy shook her head in disbelief. Her hands were shaped like claws, and her top lip curled back, showing her teeth. "I never go around the neighborhood screeching and going through trash cans! That's a lie!"

Grandma gave her a disapproving frown and shook her head side to side, letting her know that she shouldn't show catlike behavior. Purdy quickly uncurled her lip and sat on her hands.

Grandma spoke and signed to Purdy, "The caller made the same statement as your first note, Persephone. You say you only shared the first note with Rowen and your mama, but the caller said they were 'a concerned citizen.' Either they were the same people who sent the first note, or they somehow read your first note."

Purdy said, "We aren't much closer to discovering why I spent the night in a cage. But I still don't think the person who reported me knew *I* was the cat."

Purdy's mama and grandmother went shopping. Purdy was left at home, going over the recent developments. She knew something disturbing was going on. First, she saw kids at school who received unkindness notes. Then she received a few notes herself. She noticed hooded characters out at night when she followed her cat, Beau. And, she saw them again just after being picked up by animal control. *None of this makes much sense!*

Later that day, Rowen met Purdy at her house. She let him in through the kitchen door. Purdy told him about her night spent with animal control and told him she had turned back into a girl in a very tiny cage.

He gasped. "That's awful, Purdy! Who would do that to you? It wasn't me."

"I know it wasn't you, Rowen. You would never do that to me. We need to come up with a plan. I can never go through this again!"

Rowen had a new strategy: "After the night you visited me as a cat, I went online to find a pet tracking device. It's simple, really. You wear it around your neck on nights when you go out. But the tricky part is that you must put it on *before* you turn into a cat."

He showed her the small disc. It was silver and looked like a pendant on a pink elastic band. "I put it on a cord that will stretch enough to fit you when you're a girl and then shrink back down to cat size. I can follow this tracker on my phone, kind of like the one we put on Henry's truck. Only, this one was made for pets. I don't need to watch your movements all the time, but I can track you down if you ever go missing again."

"Let me see that," said Purdy. Rowen handed the device to Purdy, who stretched the cord around her neck.

"Let's try it out," said Purdy. " I'll walk around to the back of the house and hide, and I want you to find me." Purdy decided to hide inside the potting shed in her backyard.

It only took Rowen a few minutes to follow the signal, wheel his chair up to the door of the shed, and find her. "I found you, Purdy!"

Purdy came out of her hiding place with a big smile on her face. She placed both hands over the device adoringly. "I sure wish I'd had this last night!"

Chapter 21
Planning a Spy Trip

Purdy knew, through her nighttime spy trips, that Elenore and Sophie were sending out unkindness notes, but she still didn't know if her sisters were involved.

Grandma and Rowen encouraged her to go out as a cat and investigate Elenore. "Let's see if you can find any more clues," said Rowen.

"Okay," she said reluctantly. "You do remember what happened to me last time?"

"Yes, Purdy," said Rowen. "You were on your own when you got picked up by animal control. But this time you'll have backup. You won't have to worry as long as you're wearing the GPS tracker."

At 7:30 p.m., a green light flashed in Purdy's room, indicating that someone was ringing the doorbell. She ran down the stairs to answer it. Her grandmother stood outside the door with her suitcase. "Grandma, what are you doing here?"

Grandma spoke and signed, "Hello, dear. Your mom and dad are going out for the evening, and I've agreed to stay with you tonight. I'm not leaving anything up to chance after you spent a night in a cage. I've come prepared for a sleepover."

"But Grandma, Rowen has me on a GPS tracker, and I'm about to investigate. . ."

"Yes, dear, and I'm your additional backup. Let's go to your room and have a slumber party."

They reached Purdy's room, and she bent down to pull out the full-size trundle bed stored under her own bed. "Here you go, Grandma. I have it already made up in case of an unexpected sleepover."

Grandma continued to speak and sign, "I brought snacks. Eating before you turn into a cat is important, just in case your enhanced sense of smell tempts you to eat something disgusting while you are out at night." Both Purdy and Grandma wrinkled their noses at the thought.

"Uh, okay," said Purdy. "I wish I had known that sooner, Grandma. The first night I turned into a cat, I pictured my pet Cookie between two slices of bread."

Grandma's mouth hung open, and she raised her hands to her sides with hands facing upward, in a what were you thinking pose. "You didn't?"

Purdy said, "I didn't eat her, Grandma. But I almost did!"

Facing Purdy, Grandma said, "Let me tell you. One morning, I woke up with a dead mouse beside me in my bed!"

Purdy gulped. "Okay, Grandma. I'm glad you're here to teach me!"

Purdy sent a quick text to Rowen.

R.   My grandma is here and says she's going to Elenore's house with me. She tells me she's my backup plan. P

Grandma instructed Purdy to pick out a nightgown and lay it flat on her bed. Grandma did the same. Facing Purdy, she said, "That way, when we return as cats later tonight, we can just slip into them and wake up fully dressed!"

Grandma is taking my training very seriously! "Thanks, Grandma!"

At 8:30, Purdy's parents knocked on her bedroom door. Mama signed, "Oh, Mom, you're here! I thought I heard voices coming from Persephone's room. Good, good. Honey, we are going out for the night and won't be home until tomorrow morning. You two have fun and feel free to order pizza. Maybe you can even watch a movie, if you like." Mama crossed the room and hugged each of them.

Dad came in too and gave them each a hug. He signed, "Well, this looks like a fun sleepover. I hope you aren't planning a night out on the town."

Purdy smirked, "Yes, Dad. That's exactly what I'm planning. A night out with my grandma. Don't worry about us. We'll be fine!"

"Okay, then we will see you both tomorrow," said Dad, facing Purdy.

Mama waved to get Purdy's attention. "Have a great time,"

It was still early, and Purdy knew they wouldn't leave the house until they both turned into cats for the night. The last few times she had gone out at night alone, unexpected things happened. So, she was excited to have Grandma join her.

Purdy received a text from Rowen at 9:00 p.m., just an hour before cat time.

Hi Purdy, I know you have the tracking device, and your grandmother is with you for backup, but you can also expect me.

"Really, Rowen?" Purdy texted back.

You're coming too?

Rowen texted:

I convinced my dad to take me to Elenore's house and let me use his night vision goggles and camera, just in case we see someone suspicious tonight.

Purdy texted back:

That's great, Rowen! How did you convince him?

Rowen answered,

Well, I talked to him about the mystery we're trying to solve, and I also told him you'll be spying there along with your grandma.

He paused, then wrote,

My dad is always eager to use some of his spy gadgets. So, we'll be watching from the car, not too far away.

Purdy texted:

This is exciting, Rowen. Talk to you soon. P.

They said goodbye and ended the text. But not much later, Purdy received another text from Rowen.

P. Remember to put on your tracking device before leaving the house. Everything should be fine

> since you'll be a cat, and no one knows who you are.
> Best of luck! I hope we find some great clues! R.

Purdy answered Rowen's text.

> Yes, Rowen, thank you so much. I already have this
> thing around my neck. We'll be on the prowl very
> soon! P.

Facing Purdy, Grandma gave her some last-minute instructions before they both turned into cats: "Persephone, you go to the door and meow, while I keep my ears open outside. Don't worry; Rowen and I will be on the alert. Just go in and see what you can find out."

At 10:00 pm, Grandma and Purdy morphed into cats: Purdy became a black-and-white tuxedo cat, and Grandma became a long-haired calico.

Purdy peeked through her bedroom cat door, looked up and down the hallway, and spotted her sister Tara talking on her phone outside her room. When Tara finally returned to her room, Purdy and Grandma maneuvered through the cat door, down the stairs, and out the kitchen door. Street-lights and lawn lights lined the way up to the large, red brick house, two streets over.

Purdy had never been inside Elenore's house, but her mama had dropped her sisters off a few times while Purdy was in the car. A sign on the porch read 'Knight,' so she knew this was the right place. A few lights shone through the front windows. Purdy leaped up the front steps to the concrete porch and began her routine of meowing outside the door.

Grandma headed for a watching post behind a large tree. The porch light went on, just as a dark figure crossed the grass, looked straight at Purdy on the porch, and quickly hid in the shadows of the same tree where Grandma hid.

Could that be Elenore?

BAND!
ELENORE
SIMON
JACK
PACO
JORDAN
COLE
SOPHIE
TEISHA
KIM
ISABELLA
JILLIAN
ELENORE

Chapter 22
Elenore's Room

Purdy waited on the porch, and the next time she peered into the yard, she saw two hooded figures. The door to the house creaked open, and a woman in a nightgown gazed down at Purdy.

This must be Elenore's mom.

The woman said something Purdy couldn't understand, held up her hand, and then closed the screen door. Purdy was about to look for another entrance when she noticed that Elenore's mom hadn't closed the front door. Purdy waited outside for her to return.

A girl named Bonnie, a few years younger than Purdy, came to the door wearing a nightgown and carrying a saucer of milk. She set the milk just inside the front door and welcomed Purdy inside.   Purdy lapped up the milk, becoming aware of her surroundings. The woman didn't return. Bonnie petted the top of Purdy's head a few times before holding out her hand so Purdy could lick her. She felt a contented purr deep in her throat.

I didn't know this would be so easy. Bonnie picked up the empty saucer, and Purdy followed her into the kitchen. Then, Purdy followed Bonnie up the steps and into a bathroom, where Bonnie brushed her teeth. This was a Jack and Jill bathroom with two doors leading to separate bedrooms. Purdy peeked into a room with the lights on, which looked like it belonged to Bonnie. Though dimly lit, the other room had band posters and an award shelf, which looked like it might belong to Elenore.

While Bonnie was in the bathroom, Purdy scooted into Elenore's room. *I may have a minute to scope things out.* Jumping onto Elenore's desk, Purdy pawed through some papers. She noticed an envelope addressed to Elenore from The Unkindness Club. The current list of members lay flat beneath the envelope, rather than the unkind note Purdy expected. She pawed at the envelope, moving it out of her way.   She quickly read through the list.   Simon   Jack   Paco   Jadan   Cole   Sophie   Trisha   Kim   Isabella   Jillian   Elenore.   *Hey, I recognize two of the names. Elenore, who lives here, and Sophie, the girl who lost her St. Christopher necklace.*

Next to this list was a target message with yesterday's date. Purdy saw nothing on that note indicating that The Unkindness Club would lure her or her cat to the park. In another letter, she noticed Elenore had signed the words "A Concerned Citizen," just like the note Purdy received. *So, it's Elenore who signs her notes that way. She's been spying on my family!*

Bonnie came in to fetch her.

I wish I had more time to read the last note. I wonder what they have planned for tonight.

Bonnie picked Purdy up, squeezing her around the middle and holding her in her arms with her back legs and tail hanging down. Bonnie spoke to Purdy, but the little deaf cat couldn't hear what she said. She imagined the girl saying, "There you are, you rascal."

She would need to bide her time until she could leave Elenore's house. With Purdy still in her arms, they entered Bonnie's room through the joined bathroom, but the door leading to the hallway was closed. Bonnie sat on her bed with the little cat on her lap. Purdy began to meow, trying to communicate, but failing. Bonnie put her face closer to Purdy's, and Purdy read her lips. "What do you want, little cat?" Purdy meowed, jumped from the bed, and began to scratch the door.

This will probably break all my fingernails.

Bonnie got up and opened the door. Purdy then ran down the stairs and meowed at the front door. Bonnie followed her and probably said something to Purdy, which she couldn't hear. She assumed Bonnie said, "But you just got here." Or "I want to keep you. Can't you stay?"

Reluctantly, shaking her head, Bonnie opened the front door and let Purdy outside. Not looking back, Purdy leaped from the porch and ran to the tree where she found the calico cat she knew as her grandmother. She also spotted Rowen and his dad in their car nearby.

It was getting late, and Purdy was tired. Elenore wasn't in her room, so she must have been the dark figure she spotted earlier, outside the house. Information circled in Purdy's head, with no way to communicate with Grandma.

The two cats left Elenore's property. Their small feet carried them along the sidewalk for two blocks toward Purdy's light brick home.

Purdy thought, *How can I remember all those names? Their last names weren't listed. Elenore wrote the Concerned Citizen note, but why? What has my family done to upset Elenore? Or this group?*

They returned to Purdy's house and entered her bedroom. Each cat retreated to their own bed and slipped into the nightgowns they had laid out earlier. They would have to wait until morning to discuss what they found.

After an adventurous night, the cats turned back into a girl and her grandmother the next morning.

Chapter 23
Sharing Information

The doorbell rang, with the green blinking light going off in Purdy's room, and she ran to answer the front door, but no one was there. Puzzled, Purdy ran to the back door and found her friend Rowen at the door. Purdy invited him into the living room, and Grandma joined them.

"Hey Rowen, I can't wait to tell you what we found out," said Purdy.

He faced her and held up a hand, "Wait, I want to tell you first."

"Okay," said Purdy in a doubtful tone. She didn't think Rowen would have anything to say that was as important as what she had found out.

He used sign language as much as he could while speaking, "My dad drove me to Elenore's house. I could see you, Purdy, through my night-vision goggles. You were on the porch, and I saw a girl let you inside. I also saw your grandma, as a cat, under a tree near two hooded figures.

I watched for a while, then suddenly, the hooded figures ran toward the street. With my dad's night-vision camera, I got a clear picture of the two girls running toward our car." He took out the pictures to show them. One was Elenore, and they were unsure about the other girl. But their faces, in the dark, were as clear as day.

"Wow, Rowen, that's great!" said Purdy.

Now it was Purdy's turn to share, "I found proof that Elenore is part of The Unkindness Club! I saw a current list of members, but my sisters' names weren't on the list. I also saw a letter Elenore had written and signed: 'A Concerned Citizen'. So, she's the one who is watching my house. I wonder why she is targeting my family."

Grandma signed and spoke, "That's great information, Persephone! How did you find information without getting caught?"

"I meowed at the door, as Rowen said. Elenore's sister Bonnie let me inside. Then, while she brushed her teeth, I found the door to Elenore's room. On her desk was an envelope, a letter, and the list of Unkindness Club members."

Grandma's eyes went wide, and she shook her head in disbelief. Rowen smiled and waved his hands in the air, but neither of them spoke.

Purdy continued, "As I said, my sisters' names weren't on the membership list, which puzzles me. I saw another letter with the agenda for the night before, but there was no mention of kidnapping my cat or me from the park. I also noticed the agenda for last night. I only had a few minutes before Bonnie came in and found me, so I didn't have time to read it."

This information left Grandma and Rowen bewildered and scratching their heads.

"Hum! That is interesting," said Grandma, facing Purdy.

Rowen said, "Wow, Purdy, you found a lot of clues! If your sisters aren't in the club, and the club didn't kidnap you, then I'm unsure how we will use the information right now."

Grandma filled them in on what she witnessed the night before, while signing and speaking. "I hid behind the tree in the front yard and saw Elenore and another girl in black hooded sweatshirts."

"Did they say anything?" asked Rowen.

Grandma continued, "Yes. The girls discussed their next move, assuming their only witness was a small calico cat. One of the girls received a text and was reading instructions from her phone.

'Circle the Davis's house three times, staying in the shadows. Make sure no one is around and enter through the basement window. You need to get up to the study and find Mr. Davis's test scores. Find the one that says Sophie Olsen, and change the score from an F to a B+. Don't leave anything behind. When your mission is complete, sneak out through the basement window and check in with your phone to let me know you're finished. I will then text you your next assignment.'"

"Oh, wow!" said Purdy. They aren't just spying and sending threatening notes; now they're cheating. What should we do?"

Grandma said, "We know one of the girls was Elenore, but we also know the other girl was not Sophie, since she's the one who sent the text."

Purdy and Rowen nodded.

Grandma continued. "It's too soon to act on this, Persephone. We know their intentions for last night, but we don't know if these two girls broke into the teacher's house. Once we know for sure, then I think I may send a few notes myself."

"But at least we know the last name of their leader, Sophie Olsen!" said Rowen, facing Purdy, "We could talk to Henry, the delivery guy, to see if he knows anything about the Olsen family."

Rowen paused, then said, "We sure do make a great team!"

"Yes, we do," said Grandma, and Purdy nodded in agreement.

Chapter 24
Finding Answers in Her Sister's Room

Still shaken about being kidnapped and trying to process the information she found at Elenore's house, Purdy didn't venture from her home the next night.

Sunday night, just before ten, Purdy pulled the stretchy cord around her neck and lay across her bed.

Although she didn't see her sisters' names on The Unkindness Club membership list, she still had suspicions. For one, Kara took a picture of her as a cat, and last week she recorded her sisters saying they planned to put out cat treats and catch her as a cat.

For tonight, Purdy would search for answers in her own home. Once she became a cat, Purdy peeked her head out through the cat door from her bedroom. The hallway was clear, so she walked to her sisters' room across the hall. Tara had set out a bowl of milk and a few cat treats near their bedroom door. The idea of eating cat snacks had repulsed her as a girl; however, as a cat, she decided to try one. *Hey, this tastes pretty good!*

I'll take my time and see if my sisters will come out. If I let them catch me, I can get inside their room.

Tara came through her bedroom door and spotted Purdy, as a cat, eating a snack. She picked up Purdy and held her close, looking her in the eye. Purdy could read her lips from that position.

"I gotcha! You'll see, it's great in my room. You can have all the treats you want. I'm going to put a tag on you and claim you as my own." Tara pulled a round, gold disc from her pocket and clipped it onto Purdy's cat collar. "See, I'm going to name you Rosie. This tag also has my phone number, just in case you ever get lost."

Tara continued talking to Purdy. "I will take such good care of you, that you'll never miss our sister, Persephone." Tara cradled the small tuxedo cat in her arms, not knowing the cat was her younger sister. She carried Purdy into her bedroom and closed the door behind her.

In this room, there was a fireplace and matching queen-size canopy beds. Most of the furnishings were pink or white. Her sisters even had a small refrigerator in their room and a hot tub on their balcony.   Each sister wore a fluffy pink robe and had their hair up in a towel. They quickly removed the robes and towels, and they were fully clothed with their long auburn hair perfectly dry. After shaking their hair into place, it was already fluffed and styled. Tara stood in front of a mirror, putting on her lipstick. Purdy focused on reading her lips through the mirror.

"I can't take too many more late nights, Kara. Friday night nearly did me in."

Her sisters continued to chat back and forth, but Purdy could only make out a few words. She caught her own name a few times and the word Grandma.

"Kara, go check – ---- – — ride – ----."   Kara left the room, shutting the door so Purdy couldn't escape.

Purdy sat on a bed and watched. Kara came back and nodded. Both sisters left their room and went down the stairs, and then she felt a slight vibration as the front door closed.

Now, it's time to snoop around. Another vibration shook the bed where she sat. This time, Purdy realized that one of her sisters had left her phone behind.

Purdy read a text message from Jennifer on the phone.

> Hey, are you coming? It's time to meet up with the others to compare notes. We'll wait in the grassy area of the city park.

No, it can't be! Are they out delivering notes! Is it possible that my sisters sent themselves notes to shake off suspicion? I don't know what that means now that I know their names weren't on The Unkindness Club list.

Purdy jumped from the bed, ran across the room, and leaped onto their desk, where she spotted a pen with the initial T and a notepad. There were indentations on the paper where a note had been written.

With her improved eyesight, Purdy read the impressions of words:

> *P,   I have a solution for your unlicensed pet problem. Meet me at the park tonight at 11:00 p.m. and bring your cat. R.*

This is it! Here's proof that my sister Tara sent the note that could have ruined my life and changed everything. Why would she do that to me?

She spotted the unkindness notes sent to her sisters. *They weren't lying about this.* The notes had pictures. One was of Kara getting off the bus with dollar bills still waving in her hand. The other picture was of Tara kissing her new boyfriend, Kevin.

This doesn't make sense. Who would take pictures, print them, and send them to themselves?

Strewn across the back of a chair, Purdy saw a black hoodie like the one she saw someone wearing a few nights before while she was being abducted by animal control. Another black hoodie was sticking out under the first one.

They didn't wear any black tonight. So... Wait a minute! Let me read the phone message again.

Purdy returned to the bed and found that the screen had gone black. She tapped the screen with a paw, hard enough to make the message reappear. She re-read the message.

It didn't say send out notes; it said compare notes. Could I be wrong about my sisters? But wait, this is confusing. There's still an incriminating note written by my sister Tara.

Chapter 25
Does Any of this Make Sense?

The patio door in her sister's room was open a crack. She could escape their room by squeezing her small cat body through the opening.

I'm not waiting here to see what my sisters will do next.

Just before she jumped from the bed, the phone vibrated again. She checked the message.

Kara, if you haven't left yet, please bring a ruler and markers to make the rally signs. You'd better ask your parents if you can stay out late tonight. There are a lot of posters to make, and half the group didn't show up. J.

I need to get out of here before my sisters come back. I also need to contact Grandma. As a cat, I can't take pictures of the notepad. I can't even tear off the page and carry it with me. Grandma is my only hope.

If my grandma comes into my sister's room, she'll see the indentation of the letter they sent to me. She can also see the black hoodies, which my sisters must have worn on the night of my abduction.

Purdy jumped from the bed and took off. Standing on her back legs and stretching out, she managed to squeeze through the opening in the patio door and climb down the vines on the side of the house. She was careful not to disturb the vines on her way down. Purdy reached the ground and scampered to the backyard, where she could let herself back inside the house through the cat door in the kitchen.   Purdy reentered the house and skidded across the polished floor to the staircase. She jumped the steps two at a time. She then went through the cat door to her bedroom and fell asleep waiting to feel the vibrations of her sisters coming home.

The next morning, after becoming a girl, Purdy got dressed, combed her hair, and left her room. She stood outside her two sisters' door. She heard sounds and felt vibrations coming from their room. They didn't know that Persephone had been trapped in their room the night before. Once again, they thought they were trapping her cat.

Chapter 26
What's Our Next Step?

Purdy texted Rowen and Grandma to meet at the park near the pavilion. That way, they could have a private meeting and discuss all the events from the past few nights. She looked in one direction to see Rowen coming down the sidewalk in his electric wheelchair and taking the ramp, entering the park's sidewalks. When he was almost there, she turned to see her grandmother driving up in her black convertible with the top closed.

"Grandma, Rowen, I wanted to catch you up on the things I've discovered." They nodded, and she continued. "First, a few days ago, I recorded my sisters talking about me having too many cats and that they wanted to catch me. So, I assumed they were the ones who sent me the note about having too many unlicensed pets. I also thought they were in The

Unkindness Club and were sending the notes to kids at school and around the neighborhood. I really thought the name Unkindness Club matched my two sisters, since they are unkind to me and call me a pest most of the time."

Her grandmother folded her arms across her chest and shook her head back and forth. "It's such a shame, though."

"I know," said Purdy. "I put two and two together when I saw my sister's friend, Elenore, passing out notes. Remember the night I read a note that had fallen to the ground? It was signed by The Unkindness Club." Rowen faced Purdy and spoke up, "Do you still think your sisters are part of The Unkindness Club, Purdy?"

"Yes, I do, and I don't."

"What do you mean by that, dear?" asked Grandma, while signing.

"Remember when we visited Elenore's house?" asked Purdy. Grandma nodded. "That night I found a list of Unkindness Club members, but my sisters' names weren't on the list."

Grandma said, "That's true. But why do you still think your sisters might be members? Remember, they also received unkind notes."

"Yes, they did," said Purdy.

"Have you seen their notes, Purdy?" asked Rowen.

"Yes, said Purdy, "And that's another thing. Last night, I let my sisters catch me, as a cat, and take me into their room."

Rowen tried to interrupt. "But Purdy. . .

Purdy held up a hand in a stop sign position, stopping Rowen. "If you hold on, I will explain. A few things happened when I was in their bedroom. For one, I knew my sisters were talking about me. I caught my name and Grandma's name, but I couldn't hear their conversations at the time."

"But did you find any clues in your sisters' room?" asked Rowen.

"Yes, Rowen, I saw a notepad with indentations from a note. It was the note that told me to meet them at the park and to bring my cat. And it was signed R."

Rowen flung his arms in the air and gasped. Grandma folded her arms and shook her head.

"Grandma, my sisters may not be in The Unkindness Club, but they did send me at least one note. And . . . I also saw two black hoodies on a chair near their desk."

Grandma said and signed, "But you couldn't gather proof while you were a cat. Is that right, dear?"

"Right, I couldn't grab the note or even let anyone know what I found. Grandma, will you go into their room and check on those things?"

"Yes, dear, that's a great idea. I think I'll go right away."

"Do you want to visit as their grandma or as a cat?" asked Purdy.

Grandma spoke and signed, "I'll go as their grandmother and ask about the note directly. I'll say that I know they're the ones sending out unkind notes, and I wonder why they would do that to people they hardly know, and especially to their sister. They might deny it, but then I'll tell them I know they wore black hoodies and went to the park where animal control picked up their, uh, sister's cat."

"Really?" asked Rowen. "You're just going to come right out and say that they're The Unkindness Club?"

Purdy sat quietly, nodding her head in approval.

"I will!" said Grandma. "But I won't tell them that Persephone is the cat that animal control picked up. It's time for us all to be on the same side. If they aren't The Unkindness Club, then they may know who it is. That way, they can be a part of the solution and not the problem."

Purdy stood and clapped her hands. "I like that, Grandma."

"If you can get the twins to help, we can use my tracker to follow Elenore," said Rowen.

Chapter 27
Kind Notes

Purdy walked over to Rowen's house with a stack of brightly colored paper, black markers, and scissors. Unlike The Unkindness Club, she was determined to send kind notes to people around town.   Each note would be written by Purdy and Rowen, with a few kind words, and signed The Kindness Club.

When she introduced this idea to Rowen, he was excited to be part of the new club. They each took out their phones and looked up messages of kindness. At first, Purdy cut each sheet of paper into fourths while Rowen wrote notes, and then they swapped jobs.

Rowen faced Purdy and said, "How will we deliver these notes, Purdy? And who will we give them to?"

"I don't know yet but just give me time," said Purdy. "I'll come up with something. We need to write special messages to deliver to Elenore and Sophie."

Changing the subject, Purdy said, "Rowen, you told Grandma that we can use your tracker to follow Elenore." Rowen nodded.

"But Rowen, remember when we put the tracker on Henry's delivery van?"

Rowen spoke, using some sign language, "Yes, I do. The only problem is that I never got it back. That tracker is still making trips around the city, attached to Henry's van. I sometimes lie in bed on Saturday mornings, following Henry's movements."

"Okay, we need to get it back so we can follow Elenore instead. Rowen, do you know where Henry is now?" asked Purdy.

Rowen pulled out his phone and checked the tracking app. He looked up and faced Purdy, "Yeah, well, he's gone back to the store on Standon Blvd. I guess he's either filling the van with groceries or taking a lunch break."

"Okay, let's go," said Purdy. They packed the kindness notes into a shoe box and left the house.

Rowen told Purdy, "I also want to talk to him about Sophie. He seems to know most people in town. So maybe he also knows Sophie Olson's family." Facing Purdy, he said, "We can't describe her to him, but she's probably the same age as Elenore and your sisters. And she goes to school around here. By the size of the two girls, you saw that first night... How tall do you think Sophie is?"

"I don't know, Rowen. I was a cat at the time," said Purdy. "I think she was about the same height as Elenore."

The two kids hurried to where Henry had parked his van, outside the grocery store. Purdy kept watch while Rowen drove his chair up close to the delivery van and quickly removed the tracking disc from the wheel well. He showed Purdy how dirty it was before placing it in his shirt pocket.

Purdy said, "Rowen, Henry's coming."

Rowen backed up his chair and turned to face his friend. "Henry, I thought we'd find you here. Are you in a hurry today?"

Facing Purdy, he said, "Uh, no more than usual. What's up, Rowen? Have you been able to solve the mystery?"

Rowen said, "We've found some great clues, but we need help finding a girl named Sophie Olsen. She lost something, and we need to return it."

"We also think that finding her will help us with another clue. Do you know this girl, Henry?" asked Purdy. "We think she's in high school, and she's probably the leader of The Unkindness Club. Remember the group we told you about?"

"Yes, you mean the ones who are sending out unkind notes to people around your school?" asked Henry.

"Yes, and also, to anyone around the neighborhood that they determine to be wrong doers," said Rowen, facing Purdy.

Henry motioned for the two to climb into the van and ride with him. Purdy climbed into the front seat, as before, and Rowen waited behind the van so Henry could pull out the ramp. He then rode his chair in until he was behind the front seats. Henry buckled him up, ran around to the driver's side, and climbed in.

As they rode along together, Henry faced Purdy and asked, "How did you pinpoint this club to a girl named Sophie Olsen?"

"Well," said Purdy, "I went out one night, following my cat."

"Following your cat at night?" asked Henry.

Purdy turned toward Rowen as he spoke, "It's a long story, Henry, but let's just say Persephone saw two hooded figures passing out notes. She recognized one of the girls."

"Yes," said Purdy, "And we know the other girl's name is Sophie because the next day, Rowen and I went back and found a St. Christoper's Medal in the grass."

"With the name Sophie on it," continued Rowen.

"And you want to return it to her, no questions asked?" Henry said, rubbing his chin.

"Well, yes, sort of, but our main purpose is to stop The Unkindness Club," said Rowen.

"And we want to find out more about their leader," said Purdy.

"Is it your goal to turn her in? Or do you want to send an unkind note to her and get even?" asked Henry.

Rowen was quiet for a moment. "No, we've talked about it, and we really want them to stop sending notes. We don't care about getting them in trouble."

Purdy, who had been following the conversation by listening with her hearing aids and reading lips, took over. "We would never send out notes like that, Henry. Besides, Rowen and I have been writing kind notes to send out instead."

Rowen said, "Do you know where Sophie lives, Henry?"

"Yes, I think I do. However, you can't just go and accuse Sophie of sending out notes, without proof."

"No, Henry, we've written two particularly kind notes for Elenore and Sophie, and we need your help to deliver them," said Rowen.

"How do you think I can help with that?" asked Henry.

Purdy said, "We have kind notes for each of your deliveries today." She hadn't planned to do it that way, but the whole thing suddenly made sense. "We're here to make sure Sophie's note gets into her family's grocery bag, and that Elenore Knight's note gets into her family's grocery bag. Then we can place the other notes randomly.

"What does Sophie's note say?" asked Henry.

"It says, 'Kind words lead to kind actions,'" said Purdy. "And Elenore's note says, 'One kind act will come back to you tenfold.'"

"I think I can help you with that! Those notes are neither unkind nor threatening," said Henry. "What about the other notes?" asked Henry.

"Here, you can read some of them," said Rowen.

Henry stopped the van and looked at the other notes before allowing the kids to place them in different grocery orders.

One said, 'Kindness is free. Sprinkle that stuff everywhere.' – Unknown.

Another one read, 'Choose kindness.' – Unknown.

And 'Kindness is love in action.' – Unknown.

Plus, 'Kindness costs nothing.' – Unknown.

Then, 'Kindness makes you the most beautiful person in the world.' – Unknown.

And 'Spread love everywhere you go.' – Mother Teresa

Each short note ended with The Kindness Club.

"The Unkindness Club is using light-colored envelopes for their letters, so we decided to use bright, cheerful paper for our kind notes," said Rowen.

Rowen and Purdy helped Henry put notes into one bag for each delivery order. They then handed him the shoe box with the additional notes so Henry could place them in the orders he delivered on different days.

"I can't let you know where Sophie lives, although, I'm sure you kids could figure it out for yourselves. But I can tell you that I will be delivering groceries to her home this afternoon. I will certainly deliver your note along with the grocery order."

"Thank you so much, Henry!" said Rowen.

"Yes, thanks, Henry. Try Kindness, it's much better!" said Purdy

"I agree! You kids, are on the right track." He let them out near Rowen's house and drove off to do his grocery deliveries.

Chapter 28
Enlisting Help

Grandma paid a visit to Purdy's sisters. Tara opened her bedroom door and invited her grandmother to come in. Both girls were on their phones and put up a finger to indicate that they would only be a minute.

While she waited, Grandma went straight to their desk and picked up the notepad Purdy had mentioned, along with a pencil. The girls didn't notice her using the pencil to darken the page so the indentations would show up better. She then read the message Purdy had told her about. This note had led to Purdy being picked up by animal control. Grandma then noticed the pen sitting next to the notepad had the initial 'T,' which pointed to Tara as the note writer. Grandma quickly ripped the page out and stuffed it into her pocket. She had just turned around when Kara came up beside her. Grandma then spotted the two black hoodies on the chair next to her.

"I'm sorry to make you wait," said Kara. "Tara should be off the phone any time."

"Oh, that's fine, girls. No hurry. I need to talk to both of you about some things that are going on lately and see if you're aware of a problem."

Kara gathered the hoodies from the desk chair and motioned for Grandma to sit down, while she sat on a beanbag chair. Tara came over and sat cross-legged on the floor.

"What is it, Grandma?" asked Tara."

"Girls, you may be aware that some bad notes are going around the neighborhood, and even in your own home."

"We know, Grandma," said Kara. "We each got a note like that."

Kara jumped up and went to retrieve their notes from the desk. "Mine is about me always being late for school, and that I forget to pay for my city bus ride. Tara's note says that she kissed someone else's boyfriend."

"The thing is, girls, I have a reason to think that you are involved with The Unkindness Club and that you have been sneaking out of the house to send out those notes. Are you girls part of this club?"

The twins stood, suddenly. Kara shouted, "Grandma! No! We didn't send out those notes. See? Here are the notes and the pictures we received."

Tara's mouth dropped, and she shook her head vigorously.

"Are you telling me that you didn't sneak out of the house?" asked Grandma.

"Uh, well, yes, we did do that, but we aren't involved with the club."

"Girls, I know that you wrote at least one note to your sister, Persephone. Do you recall a note that started with P. and ended with an R.? This note encouraged your sister to go to the park late at night and to bring her cat."

Tara hung her head and spoke softly. "That was me. But... I'm not in The Unkindness Club. And, I don't know who sent the other notes."

Kara said, "We saw the note that Persephone got from 'A Concerned Citizen.' Our sister has a new cat that comes and goes from her bedroom at night. She also has her other cat, Beau, and a gerbil named Cookie. There's a box full of kittens, along with a mother cat living in our backyard, just like her note said."

Grandma nodded. "And you just thought you would help her out with a solution to the cat problem?"

"Yes," said Tara eagerly. "At first I really wanted to catch the black and white cat and keep it for my own. But after Persephone brought a mother cat with six kittens to the house, we decided to call animal control."

Kara said, "We used the idea from the first note and sent a solution. We knew she would come because she thought the note was from her friend Rowen."

"Did you think that your note was harmless?" asked Grandma.

"Yes," said Tara. "It was harmless, Grandma. Her new cat got picked up by animal control, right? We saw the protection guy scoop her up in his net. So, what's the harm if her precious cat spent the night in a cage?"

Kara spoke up, "Somehow, the cat was back in the house the next night. We aren't sure why they didn't either keep it or demand a license."

They both shook their heads in wonder, their shiny waves of auburn hair swaying.

Grandma said, "You have no idea about the problems your note caused, but that's not my point here. How do you feel about the notes you received from The Unkindness Club?"

"We hate it, Grandma. That kind of note hurts people. Why does someone want to get us in trouble?" asked Kara.

"Well, I'm working on that mystery along with Persephone and Rowen. Your sister saw your friend Elenore and others passing out letters, so we assume your friend has a connection with The Unkindness Club.

"Elenore? Really?" said Tara.

"Yes, I am sure about Elenore," said Grandma.

"Rowen has a tracking device and would like for one of you to help by placing it in Elenore's backpack," said Grandma. "We're hoping she'll lead us to The Unkindness Club leader. Would you be willing to do that?"

They both consented.

"And girls, please don't mention this to Elenore or anyone else at this point."

The twins nodded in agreement.

"I have third period with Elenore Knight on Tuesdays," said Kara. "It's Monday now, so I'll do it tomorrow."

They all hugged. Then Grandma said, "That would be great, I'll have Rowen talk to you later today."

Chapter 29
The Unkindness Club

Purdy's sisters approved a plan for catching The Unkindness Club in action. Rowen gave Kara the cleaned up, round, flat tracker, which she agreed to drop into Elenore's backpack at school. Then Rowen and Purdy would follow her with the tracking app on his phone. They all hoped Elenore would lead them to those who were sending out notes around the community.

Kara came up next to Elenore's desk while they were in history class. She spoke softly, "Elenore, it seems like we never get to see you anymore. What have you been up to?"

Elenore turned red and stammered, "Uh, well, I've been busy with a new club I've joined. We should plan something together soon, don't you think?"

While Elenore had her head down and nervously fidgeted with her pen, Kara gently poked the tracker inside her half-zipped backpack.

"Yes, let's plan something soon," Kara said quietly and backed away, turning toward her seat.

After class, Kara texted Rowen and Purdy,

> It's a go!

When school was out, the tracker's GPS location began to move according to the app on Rowen's phone. Rowen and Purdy followed.

"It looks like she's walking toward the library," said Rowen.

Rowen and Purdy headed in that direction to see what was up. On their way, Purdy texted her sister.

> Thanks for placing the tracker, Kara. We're following Elenore on her way to the library. Meet us there. We'll text you if we run into any problems.

"Purdy! Over there," said Rowen facing her and pointing. "Elenore just entered a conference room at the back of the library."

"Hopefully, she led us straight to an Unkindness Club meeting," said Purdy.

"It sure helps that they're meeting in a glass room, Purdy. That way, we can see who else shows up. And you can read their lips." Purdy nodded in agreement.

Rowen drove his chair up to a bookshelf near the glass enclosure where a few older kids had gathered. He fascinated himself with a couple of books on a low shelf across from the door. Purdy stood close to him and positioned herself where she could read lips.

A girl rushed past them and entered the room. "Sorry, I'm late. – ---- — Unkindness Club meeting?"

An older girl standing at the front of the room nodded her head and indicated for the other girl to take a seat.

As she rushed to her chair, the girl continued to speak. "I'm Lilly. - — ---- ad – — internet, ------ – help those — ---- ------- bullied – get revenge. I'm ------ bullied – school, and I ----- ---- revenge. -------, there's ---- nasty, mean guy – — neighborhood — — ------ ------- trash into our yard."

Purdy turned to Rowen and said, "They're putting ads on the internet to get new members."

"I thought so," said Rowen. "Now we know for sure."

Purdy turned her attention to the meeting on the other side of the glass partition.

"I'm Sophie and I'm the club leader."

Purdy visibly gulped, remembering the name on the St. Christopher's medal she'd found. *So, Sophie is the leader.*

Sophie was saying, "Lilly, you — ------- — type of person – need. We'll---- — get even."

Sophie continued, "- — bullied by – P.E. teacher — never ------ I was ---- enough – – on a team. Nothing - — — ---- good enough. It's ---- worse – home! I ---- — older brothers — — treated ---- kings, while - ---- do all the work ------ — house."

Sophie's face turned bright red, her mouth moved more exaggeratedly, and she pounded her fist on a table. I'll show them! I will show all of them!"

Purdy thought her voice must be rising in pitch.

Sophie began to gain her composure. "If anyone ---- — injustice, please report – — – will handle – – this group."

Another girl raised her hand. One of the other kids said impatiently, "Yes, and who are you?"

They don't even seem to be kind to the other people in their club, thought Purdy.

"I'm Kim. I – ----- accused – cheating – - test. After I got 100%,- — sent to the principal's -----. — everyone is turning against me. I ---- want to get even."

A grin played across Sophie's face. "I have an idea ---- ---- — can do that!"

An older boy Purdy didn't recognize got up and closed the door.

Rowen snapped his fingers, turned toward Purdy and said, "Dang! Now we can't hear anything inside the meeting! But I may have heard enough."

Rowen and Purdy remained near the enclosure. "They're planning something for tonight!" said Purdy, who was reading their expressions and their lips.

"Sophie asked, 'Who's in?' and several hands went up."

Sophie then demonstrated what an all-black outfit should look like. She held up her own black tee-shirt, socks, shoes, and pants, and wrote on the board,

'**The all-important black hoody!**'"It ---- – a hoody so you can cover ---- hair — ---- your face in shadow.

We don't want – – recognized," The leader said.

Sophie continued to talk while she wrote on the chalkboard.

☐ **Most crucially, you need to sneak out of the house.**

☐ **We put out the notes, and now we get results.**

☐ **Jadan, Jack, and Trisha, take the Franklin house. Look for a box of kittens.**

☐ **Jack, watch for the black and white cat. Take pictures.**

☐ **Kim, Jillian, Paco, and Cole put notes on doors.**

> **▫ I'll go with Elenore, Isabella, and Lilly. We'll check the next block**
>
> **▫ Our Goal: Find some mischief!**

The club members frantically wrote down their assignments, then she quickly erased the board.

At the end of the meeting, they all came together in a circle.

Purdy could only see one face clearly as everyone put their hands in the air and said, "We are The Unkindness Club."

Purdy became so involved in watching the group that she didn't notice as one girl and one guy casually walked over and opened the door; they each grabbed Purdy by an arm and brought her into the room. In front of the group.

The girl asked Purdy, "Were you listening to our meeting?"

The leader, Sophie, said, "That was quick thinking, Trisha, and Cole. I think she's a spy!"

She's right! I am a spy and they caught me.

Purdy lifted her hair, pointed to a hearing aid, and said, "I can't hear anything you say. I didn't know you were talking to me."

Rowen texted Purdy's sisters,

> SOS, come quickly! They caught P. and took her into their meeting!

Tara and Kara were in their car outside the library, ready to pick up Persephone and Rowen, in case they needed to make a quick getaway.

Both sisters entered the library, where one sister walked into the glass room, put her hands on her hips and said, "Oh, there you are, little sister. We came to pick you up. Did you find the book you were looking for?"

Purdy held up the random book she had picked up outside the conference room.

Her other sister stood back, looking as if she was also waiting for Rowen and Purdy, but instead, she was writing down the names of those she could recognize inside the glass enclosure. When Purdy and her sister came out, each twin grabbed Persephone by an arm and guided her to the check-out desk with her book. They then left the library together and went out to the car. Rowen left in a different direction and met them in the parking lot.

They compared notes. Tara knew most of the club members, adding last names to the list, and Kara knew the rest.

Unable to transport Rowen's chair in their car, Purdy's sisters gave her a ride home, while Rowen rode home in his chair.

Rowen's plan to place the tracker paid off. Now that they had the names of the club members, they could proceed with a plan to stop them from targeting others with their notes.

Chapter 30
Kindness Works Better

The next day after school, Purdy sent a group text to Rowen, Grandma, and her twin sisters.

We know The Unkindness Club is looking for new members with a message of revenge. It's time for us to put a complete stop to this. It's time for us to use the information we have for a good cause. Please meet me at Rowen Carter's home at 4:00 p.m. The Kindness Club.

Later, when they arrived at Rowen's house, he welcomed each of them at his back door and led the way to the living room. Purdy's heart beat faster when she saw one of Rowen's dogs walk by. Sensing her uneasiness, his mother gave her a questioning look, but she put the dogs in the basement and closed the door.

Purdy's Grandmother sat at the front of the group, interpreting the words into sign language so Purdy wouldn't miss any of the conversation.

Purdy told the group, "I'm so glad you could all make it. As you know, we've been trying to solve the mystery of The Unkindness Club, because so many of us," she said, sweeping her arm around the room, "have received notes accusing us of wrongdoing. This has led us," she pointed between herself and Rowen, "to start the Kindness Club."

The twins flipped through their phones.

Purdy cleared her throat and continued, "We began the first part of our plan by putting kind notes into grocery bags. Henry, the driver for the store, then delivered them, along with groceries, on his route. We're hoping to reach some Unkindness Club members with our kind messages."

Purdy's sisters whispered among themselves.

Rowen faced Purdy and spoke up, "Henry has heard comments from store customers who are looking forward to receiving these notes, and some people have asked Henry how they can join The Kindness Club."

Purdy said, "Thanks to my sisters, we now have the first and last names of The Unkindness Club members, and if we wanted to, we could get revenge."

Grandma interrupted, still signing, "But I thought we were The Kindness Club. We aren't here for revenge, are we?"

Rowen put up a hand to stop Grandma from continuing. "No, we aren't here for revenge."

Grandma nodded in agreement.

Rowen continued, "However, since we are The Kindness Club, we want to give Unkindness members a chance to make things right and even allow them to join our group if they'd like to."

One sister raised her hand. "Yes, Kara, or Tara, I'm not sure which one you are," said Rowen.

"I'm Kara. Do we want those people to know our business after the hateful things they've been doing?"

"That's a good question, Kara," said Rowen. "They would need to make a few changes before we could accept their membership."

"A few changes!" said Tara loudly. "I'm not so sure I could ever trust them."

Purdy and Rowen nodded, and Purdy continued. "The second part of our plan is to send a note to the club leader, Sophie Olsen. In this note, we will let her know that we have uncovered her membership list. And I'll send her the list of names we came up with when we saw them at the library."

With her hands on her hips, Tara said, "But our names won't be on that note, will they? Remember, this is a group that wants revenge. Who knows what they would do to us if they knew we were behind this note?"

"No," Purdy reassured her. "We'll tell their leader that if they choose kindness, we won't release the list of names to those who received the unkind notes. Our names won't be on the note; it will be signed: The Kindness Club."

"Okay," said Kara and Tara together.

Rowen said, "Persephone, your grandma, and I have been trying to solve this mystery for a while now, and we have other forms of evidence against this group."

"Oh, really?" asked Kara, standing with both hands raised in a I can't believe it sign.

"Yes," said Purdy. "The night when I noticed Elenore sending out notes, I also saw another person drop something onto the ground. The next day, Rowen and I found a St. Christopher medallion that Sophie dropped."

"And I have photos of two girls in black hoodies—from a different night—taken with my dad's night vision camera," said Rowen.

"Oh, wow, we underestimated you two. I'm so glad you let us in on your scheme. We really want to stop The Unkindness Club," said Tara.

"Yes, they are both very clever," said Grandma, with a huge grin.

Purdy read the note she and her grandma wrote to Sophie, aloud to their small group:

Dear Sophie Olsen

Unkindness Club Leader

We understand that your group has been targeting people you've labeled as wrongdoers, but we believe you and your group are the actual wrongdoers. The name of your group, The Unkindness Club, says it all, because you are unkind.

We are also aware of your plans to break into Mr. Davis's house to change your grade from an F to a B+.

We know about your club and its harmful intentions.

We also know what you're planning next.

We've found this St. Christopher medallion with your name on the back. This metal and a witness can prove that you were involved in sending out the unkind notes.

With this letter, we are asking you to end your plans for revenge and join the Kindness Club to help the community.

However, if your group chooses to continue with unkind acts, we will share this list of names with everyone who has received unkindness notes.

Try Kindness—it's much better.
The Kindness Club

Here's a list of your current club members :
Simon Perkins
Isabella Blake
Jadan Tracker
Sophie Olsen
Trisha Ricks
Kim Sampson
Paco Gonzoles
Elenore Knight
Jack Ross
Cole Ramsey
Jillian Summers
and a new member, Lily Bradley.

"That's great, Purdy. One more thing." Rowen pulled out the pictures he had taken outside Elenore's house. "We need to add these to the letter." He took a sticky note from the end table and wrote in marker:

"We have pictures, and pictures don't lie."

They placed the items, along with the letter, in a bright green envelope and sealed it.

Rowen planned to give the letter to Henry for delivery the next day.

Chapter 31
The Kindness Club

Rowen and Purdy continued their meeting after Grandma and the twins left Rowen's house.

"The third part of our plan is to hold a Kindness Club event and invite those who've received Unkindness notes," said Purdy. "If everything goes as planned, both groups will come together as a group, where no one knows who wrote the notes, and everyone will believe they were there for the same purpose."

Rowen said, "Both groups can come together in friendship with an atmosphere of fun, in a way that helps the community."

Purdy agreed. "We need to involve others in this plan, Rowen. We can't do this alone. Let's see if the school can help. Will you call the school principal and set up a meeting?"

Rowen nodded. He looked up the school phone number and made the call. Purdy didn't hear the conversation.

After the call, he said "Yes! You have a meeting with Mr. Harvey tomorrow after school."

A big smile crossed Purdy's face, "That's great Rowen. So far our plan is working!

Right after school the next day, Rowen waited outside the office while Purdy approached Mr. Harvey with a plan.

When she entered the office, the principal stood and shook her hand. "Miss Franklin, I hear you have a matter you wish to discuss with me. How can I help?"

"Mr. Harvey, may I have your permission to record our conversation?"

"Yes, yes of course."

Purdy turned on her recorder and then spoke. "Mr. Harvey, have you heard about a group calling themselves The Unkindness Club?"

"Yes, Miss Franklin, I'm aware. Many of our students and half the staff here at the Bedford Elementary School have received these notes. Have you also received a note, Miss Franklin?"

"Yes, yes, I did!"

"I'm so sorry to hear that. "I have no idea who is sending them out, nor do I know how we can stop them," said Mr. Harvey, facing Purdy.

"That's exactly why I'm here, Mr. Harvey. She walked to the door and stuck her head out. "Rowen, you can come in now."

Rowen entered the wide door to the office in his motorized chair.

"Well, Mr. Carter, I'm so glad you could join us." The principal stood and walked toward Rowen. He shook his hand and then returned to his seat.

Rowen said, "Purdy, I mean Persephone, and I have been working to solve the mystery of the Unkindness Club. We know who was sending out those letters. We also know why they did it."

"But who and why then?" asked Mr. Harvey.

"Wait a minute," said Purdy. "It was never our goal to turn in the wrongdoers and get them in trouble, Mr. Harvey. We want to stop the notes from going out. And we have a plan to do that."

Mr. Harvey stood, "But I need to know who did this and why they did it!"

Rowen raised a hand. "Please hear us out, Mr. Harvey, and I think you will like our plan."

Sitting back down, the principal said, "Okay, I'll listen to your plan."

Purdy spoke up. "Mr. Harvey, instead of reporting The Unkindness Club, we plan to have a neighborhood party, including all the people who have received unkindness notes, along with those who sent out the notes. That way, no one will know one group from the other."

"Yeah," said Rowen. "We started a group of our own, and we're calling ourselves The Kindness Club."

"Oh really," said the principal, leaning forward in his chair. "I'm listening, and this is getting interesting."

"Okay," continued Purdy. "This plan includes the elementary school, the junior high, and the high school. We need help from the community to bring in food, several bouncing houses, and maybe a pony ride."

Rowen continued, facing Purdy. "We'll take donations at the door. The admission will be one blanket, and this can be for a baby, a homeless pet, or for older people who live in a nursing home."

Facing Purdy, the principal said, "I, I like it so far! Yes, that's it exactly. A community event that helps others and involves all three schools. We end this now! We turn it all around, and we won't let one group be singled out or punished. Instead, they all come together, and donations will go to a good cause. I will contact the other schools right now."

Purdy stood and Rowen turned to go.

"One more thing," said Purdy, whose mind was racing, "Mr. Harvey, we need to do this right away, so The Unkindness Club will end, and the Kindness Club will take over."

"When were you thinking, Miss Franklin?"

"We would like to have the party in two weeks on a Saturday," Purdy said

"Well, yes. If we get all the schools together on this, we can pull it off."

"That will be Saturday, September 20th. Let's plan it for the middle of the afternoon. So that's from 2:00 to 5:00," said Rowen.

They all agreed on the plans they made, and the principal shook their hands. They said their goodbyes, and Mr. Harvey said, "Thank you both! I'll let you know."

"Okay," said Purdy. "We'll start getting the word out."

Purdy left the office, and Rowen followed as she found a quiet room, next to the office, where she could hook up her hearing aids and listen to the whole conversation.

Chapter 32
Our Plans Have Been Compromised

Letter

Sophie Olson received a letter from a group calling itself The Kindness Club. It arrived in a bag of groceries delivered from the Big Y store.

Sophie's plans had been going so well. She'd found a way to change her grades from an F to a B+. But then, everything she had worked for began to unravel.

First, the girls she assigned to break into Mr. Davis's house and change her grades had failed. They had said. 'This is crossing the line, Sophie. We are not cheaters; we're the ones exposing cheaters, and now you expect us to do this!'

Then she received a letter asking her to Try Kindness.

Sophie spoke to her poodle, Candy. "But why? I'm a leader. People follow me and do what I ask."

But that was not all. Someone had found her St. Christopher's medallion and sent it back to her in the same bright green envelope. She reached up to her neck to feel if her necklace was missing. Sophie found that her medallion no longer hung from her neck. This necklace was hers, but she had no idea how or where they had found it.

Sophie poured it from the envelope. She turned the medal over in her hand before placing it back around her neck.

She petted her dog and said, "You are such a good girl! At least you love and understand me. I know the note was right. I know kindness would be a much better way."

She spoke a little louder then, "This Kindness Club has a list of our club members. So, for now, we'll need to lay low; otherwise, they'll release those names. And now they even have pictures of two of our club members in dark hoodies!" Her voice continued to rise in pitch. "The note they sent said, 'Pictures Don't Lie!' That was our line. They are using my tactics against me now!"

Her pet was there to comfort her a few days later, when she received a second note. This one also arrived in a grocery bag. Candy licked her face, and she stroked her dog as she opened the bright pink envelope and read the newest letter.

Club members:

It has been brought to our attention that our members' names and our club activities have been compromised. Through our past activities, we've found that being unkind to others isn't the best way to solve our problems. Instead, we will be trying something new. There will be a party on Saturday, September 20th, at 2:00 p.m. in the junior high school gym to celebrate friendship.

Let's try kindness—it works better.

Signed, The New Kindness Club

"It appears that someone else is taking over my group, but who?" said Sophie. "Or does that even matter? The Unkindness Club members will assume this letter was from me, their leader. I didn't send out this letter, and besides, I received one myself."

Chapter 33
Apologies

After receiving a second note from Rowen and Purdy, Sophie called her last Unkindness Club meeting. The purpose of this meeting was to send apology notes to those affected. She texted her members, asking them to meet with her at the public library. She set out pastel paper and pens with different colors of ink and waited.

After her club members arrived, Sophie stood before her group and said, "The purpose of this meeting is to write notes of apology to those who were upset by our Unkindness Club letters."

A few girls stood up and headed for the door. "No, no," said Sophie, "We're all in this together. This is the very last Unkindness Club meeting. After this, you can choose kindness if you wish. But it starts by writing our apologies so we can have a fresh start."

The girls returned to their seats and began writing notes along with the others in the room.

The room became very quiet as they wrote their apologies.

The next day, Purdy and her sisters received handwritten notes on pastel paper, taped to their front door.

To Kara,

I know you are busy supporting the football team, and working to keep your grades up at school. Your mind was somewhere else when you forgot to pay for the bus. We have learned that you have since paid for all the bus fares you have missed.

Thank you for your service to the your school.

Trying out Kindness.

Purdy's note said:

Persephone Franklin,

It has been pointed out to us that you took in too many cats to save their lives.

Kittens of that age do not require a license.

Thank you for your community service!

Trying out Kindness!

The other notes were anonymous, but Tara received a personal note signed by the sender.

Tara Franklin.

I wrote you an unkind note after I saw you kissing a boy I liked, and I felt like it was unfair.

He is not my boyfriend, but I wish he were. Now I'm sorry that I wrote that letter.

Elenore Knight

P.S.: But if you bring this up, thinking you'll try to embarrass me, I will deny it. I hope we can still be friends.

The notes Purdy and Rowen sent to The Unkindness Club leader and its members worked, and the apology notes proved that Sophie had a change of heart.

Even schoolteachers received apologizes from Sophie and her group.

In a letter to the high school principal, Sophie wrote:

Dear Ms. Faulkner,

We have been causing problems for students and teachers. We thought we had been mistreated and misunderstood, but now we realize we've gone too far. If we aren't getting passing grades, we will need to work harder and earn better grades, rather than assuming our teachers hate us. From now on, instead of being students with the worst grades, we'll volunteer for extra credit, and our grades will soar!

Trying out Kindness!

Chapter 34
Sending Invitations

P urdy's school principal, Mr. Harvey, approached her in the school hallway and asked her to follow him into his office. She turned on her recorder as he spoke to her.

"I have been in touch with the principals of the junior high and high school. The junior high principal agreed to host the party on September 20th. Each school is forming a group to oversee one aspect of the neighborhood party. Meetings will be set up with the volunteers so that you, Miss Franklin, along with Mr. Carter, can lead the discussion."

"Thank you so much, Mr. Harvey," said Purdy. Before dismissing herself and going to class.

Purdy's sisters took on the assignment of designing posters and flyers, and the next day, Purdy and Rowen helped to pass them out around the neighborhood.

Be My Neighbor!

Do you choose kindness?

Do you want to help the community?

Please come to the Neighborhood Party.

When: Saturday, September 20th, at 2:00 p.m.

In the Jr. High Gym

Where: 2021 Waslow Street.

Admission: Bring one blanket for an infant, a pet, or an older person.

Invite your neighbors, young and old, to the party sponsored by The Kindness Club.

Try Kindness, which is much better!

After a busy morning passing out notes and tacking up posters, Rowen, Purdy, Tara, and Kara hoped all their planning would pay off.

That afternoon, Purdy was speaking with volunteers at the high school. Henry Collins, the delivery driver also showed up to volunteer.

Media representatives from Channel 4 News attended the meeting.

Before they went live, the reporters interviewed several people about The Kindness Club, and everyone pointed out that Purdy and Rowen had started the whole idea.

"This is Stephanie Patrick, Channel 4 News, Salt Lake City, Utah." I'm coming to you live from The American Way Junior High School, where students and teachers are volunteering to set up a neighborhood party."

"There's a new group in town", said the announcer. "This group is called The Kindness Club. This idea started with two local kids, Persephone Franklin and Rowen Carter, who began by putting kind notes into grocery bags delivered by a local driver, Henry Collins."

The reporter then turned to Henry. "I understand that you've been sending out kind notes to your delivery customers. Will you tell us about that?"

Henry nodded, "My customers love receiving such notes along with their grocery deliveries. Many have asked how they can join the Kindness movement. This week, I will be passing out invitations to the neighborhood party. I hope everyone will participate in this worthwhile community event."

"Mr. Collins, was it your idea to send out kind notes?" asked the reporter.

"Oh, no. That was entirely the idea of Persephone and Rowen," said Henry.

"How well do you know these two kids?" asked the reporter.

"I've known Rowen Carter since he was very young. I also drive the transport for doctor's appointments, and he's one of my clients. It seems that wherever you might see one of these kids, the other is always nearby.

I have known Persephone Franklin almost as long as I've known Rowen. These are two smart kids, and when they wanted to solve the mystery of The Unkindness Club, I offered to help. That's when they devised a counterattack. They wanted to send out kind notes as opposed to the unkind letters people have received around their neighborhood and at their school."

"Thank you, Mr. Collins." The newscaster continued: "Rowen Carter came up with the theme for the neighborhood party, 'Be My Neighbor', and Persephone Franklin asks the question, 'How can people be mean to each other if they are treated like neighbors?'"

"This event will take place at the American Way Junior High School gymnasium on **Saturday, September 20th, from 2:00 to 5:00 p.m.**

Admission to this event is one blanket, which The Kindness Club will donate to a local animal shelter, a hospital NI CU, or a local nursing home. Please specify the type of blanket you are donating.

It has been brought to our attention that these two local children, aged nine and a half and ten years old, are also responsible for solving the mystery of The Unkindness Club, and that this party is being held to erase unkindness and promote kindness.

Many onlookers have noted that The Kindness Club knows who sent the notes that had this neighborhood in an uproar, but the leader of The Kindness Club, who calls herself Purdy Franklin, points out that their goal was to stop the unkind letters from being sent, and not to exact revenge. As quoted by Purdy Franklin, "Try Kindness. It is much better."

"This is Stephanie Patrick, Channel 4 News, Salt Lake City, Utah."

ASMISSION
ONE
BLANKET

Chapter 35
Be My Neighbor Party

Purdy, Rowen, Grandma, and the twins met at the junior high school gym, two hours before the neighborhood party. Volunteers from the high school basketball team showed up to set up tables and chairs around the gym. The garden club placed trees, flowers, and paper birds around the gym in a rain forest theme. The hardware store donated funds for three indoor bounce houses for younger children. The grocery store donated hot dogs, buns, and condiments. A clothing store brought in a cotton candy machine.

"Make room, make room! The quilt ladies have a huge donation!" said Grandma. "This will certainly start the ball rolling!" Grandma's quilt club donated arms full of homemade quilts to begin a collection for pets, infants, and older adults, with special donations set aside for veterans.

The junior high school staff set up booths with signup sheets for volunteer opportunities:

The Library had a signup sheet for a story time volunteer to read and do crafts with kids.

There was a signup sheet for pine cone pickup in parks and cemeteries.

The quilt club offered grab-and-go quilt kits for volunteers to piece and tie at home.

A nursing home and hospital requested help with snow removal during the winter months.

Schools and churches needed Spanish translators.

A church pastor would like to have a volunteer ASL sign language interpreter for church services.

A signup sheet was also set up for volunteers to stock books for the Little Free Library.

S.A.C.K—Supporting a Community with Kindness—needed volunteers to knit or crochet soap sacks and add a bar of soap for homeless shelters.

Volunteers were also requested at an animal shelter to foster pets, walk dogs, create gift bags for pet adopters, and participate in a Read-to-a-Pet reading program. The reader must be at least six years old and anyone under ten needed to bring a parent with them.

"Today is the big day," said Purdy. "I can't wait to see all the kindness we can spread to the community through this event!"

Purdy and Rowen were seated at a table near the gym's main door, where they could collect the blankets as people entered. Each person who donated a blanket received ten raffle tickets. The Grand Prize was a two-night stay at a Las Vegas hotel and casino.

Purdy's sisters, Kara and Tara, were assigned to the fishing well. Purdy watched people drop a fishing line into a wooden well. On the fishing line, kids received special gifts, such as coupons for ice cream cones, tacos, or hamburgers, donated by local businesses. Along with the gifts, they received notes with requests from community members who needed help. One girl received a gift card for a hamburger, along with a note that said, 'Mrs. Carmon needs you to walk her dog.' A boy received a coupon for a sub sandwich, along with a note that suggested 'Mr. Herman could use your help raking leaves.'

There were prize drawings every fifteen minutes. Everyone at the event was carrying around a stuffed pet, a reusable mug, or a bag of candy from the prize table.

Grandma and Purdy's mom gave out hot dogs and cotton candy.

Every half hour, there were performances by kids in Irish Dance, an adult Broadway-style singer, and an Elvis Presley impersonator.

The big climax was preformed by the students from the magicians' school, performing magic tricks. Purdy and Rowen were fascinated when a magician turned a girl into a squirming calico cat. But moments later, the girl reappeared and kept asking, "What happened? What happened?" while everyone else laughed.

Purdy noticed Sophie Olsen signing up as a volunteer for the animal shelter. "Look, Rowen, this girl is taking kindness very seriously."

"Look behind her, Purdy. She has her whole group signing up with her."

"I think Sophie must be a great leader, after all." Purdy could hardly suppress a giggle bubbling up in her throat. Or was it a meow?

At the end of the party, Grandma came up to the table where Rowen and Purdy sat. She held a pile of signup sheets.

"Would you look at this!" Grandma said, "The lists for volunteers are very long!"

Purdy looked at the list of people who signed up to knit or crochet soap sacks. "There are twenty names on this list!"

Rowen said, "I want to see the list for the animal shelter." Grandma handed him the list. "Sophie and a few of her group signed up to foster pets, while others signed up to read to pets."

Grandma pointed out, "Look at all the people who have smiles on their faces!"

Purdy swept an arm out to indicate the borrowed laundry bins, piled with donated blankets. "If we stacked all the blankets, they would probably reach the ceiling!"

"I'd say this party is a success!" said Grandma. "I signed up to stock The Little Free Library with books. And your mama volunteered as a sign language interpreter for a church."

"We're going to start our own kindness project," said Rowen.

"Yeah," said Prudy. "The new Kindness Club will collect gloves, socks, and coats for homeless people."

"Oh, and sleeping bags too," said Rowen.

"That's a great idea!" said Grandma.

Purdy and Rowen stayed near the pile of collected blankets. As people left the party, they shook their hands, but the most unexpected gesture came from Sophie Olsen. As she was leaving with her group of friends, each carrying stuffed animals or bags of candy, she came up to Purdy and put a hand on her shoulder, making sure Purdy could read her lips. She said, "Thank you!"

Sophie then said something else that Purdy couldn't understand.

"What did she say, Rowen?"

"She said, 'Kindness is much better!'" said Rowen.

A look of surprise and amazement came over Purdy and Rowen's faces as their eyes followed Sophie. The leader stood to the side while each of her friends, standing single file, put a hand on Purdy and Rowen's shoulders, and also said, "Thank you!"

Purdy saw her twin sisters coming toward her. One sister, standing on each side of her, bent down and kissed her on the cheek. Kara said, "Persephone, we are very proud of you for solving this mystery."

Tara said, "Thank you, little sister. You and Rowen have really made a difference in this community."

The three sisters hugged, with Rowen in the middle of the huddle, and tears were running down each of their faces.

Grandma and her mama also came to give Purdy and Rowen a hug. Rowen's parents came and joined in hugging each of them.

As Purdy left the party with her Grandma, she said, "Grandma, being a cat isn't so bad after all." They both let out a giggle that sounded more like a meow, and quickly covered their mouths.

The party had been a major success for the neighborhood!

Days later, kids were chatting about the party at school. Adults talked about the party in line at the grocery store and at the movie theater, but there was no more mention of The Unkindness Club!

Purdy and her grandmother made occasional spy trips as cats at night around the neighborhood, but everything seemed to be in order.

The whole neighborhood had changed. There was no reason for people to sneak around in black hoodies at night or to be unkind to others. They found that kindness worked much better.

THE END

More Information About Deafness

Hearing loss can result from genetics, ear infections, noise exposure, injuries, or illnesses such as meningitis, measles, or mumps, and these can lead to permanent hearing loss.

In the case of Purdy Franklin, a fictional character, her hearing loss was caused by a case of meningitis when she was six years old. Some people are born with hearing loss, while others experience it in childhood or adulthood. Some have total hearing loss, while others benefit from hearing aids or devices called Ocular Implants.

Etiquette for communicating with a deaf person:

- Avoid covering your mouth when speaking.
- Face the person you are speaking with, so they can better read your lips.
- Treat individuals with hearing loss respectfully and as capable learners.

• To get their attention, wave or gently tap their arm or shoulder.

• If unsure how to communicate, write a note or text.

• Remember, a deaf person might seem different, but we all share more similarities than differences.

This information comes from April Tribe Giauque and Kathy Bernunzio plus:

Deaf Etiquette United Way Greater Toronto and Hearing Loss symptoms and causes—the Mayo Clinic

More Information About Spina bifida:

In this story, Rowen was born with spina bifida. This is a condition where the spinal column fails to close fully during the first month of a mother's pregnancy, causing damage to the spinal cord and nerves.

This condition can range from mild to severe, and in some cases, there may be loss of feeling in the lower body.

Etiquette for interacting with someone in a wheelchair:

• A wheelchair is like a part of a person's body and their personal space. Don't touch or lean on the wheelchair without permission.

• Speak directly to the person in a wheelchair. Don't address their caregiver. If the conversation lasts more than a few minutes, sit or kneel so that you are speaking at eye level.

• Avoid staring at the person in a wheelchair or touching their personal items.

Always ask before stepping in to help

this information comes from: Disability Etiquette Tips and Mayo Clinic: Spina bifida Symptoms and causes.

About The Illustrator:

Frankie Grant is a Deaf artist based in Idaho and the creator of Frankie's Timeless Art. As a children's book illustrator, Frankie brings stories to life through expressive, detailed artwork inspired by imagination, nature, and emotion. Frankie works closely with authors to visually interpret their stories, creating illustrations that help young readers connect with each page. He also specializes in elements of American Sign Language, celebrating Deaf culture and encouraging inclusion. Through each illustration, Frankie aims to enhance the author's vision and create a meaningful, engaging experience for readers. http://linktr.ee/Frankie.timeless

About The Author

Jill Ammon Vanderwood is an award-winning author with fifteen published books. She mostly writes for children and young adults.

Jill is the mother of four and a grandmother, living with her husband in a small town in Idaho.

Jill is making a difference for the next generation by writing about topics such as inclusion, where readers can see that we are more alike than we are different.

Jill is an active member of The Society of Children's Book Writers and Illustrators (SCBWI) and The League of Utah Writers. She loves speaking at schools and teaching workshops for other writers.

http://www.jillvanderwood.com

Bring an Author To Your School:

If you are interested in connecting with an author, consider inviting Jill Ammon Vanderwood to your school. Jill Vanderwood is an author and speaker from Idaho. Jill is willing to travel to nearby states. She loves to visit schools for author nights, classroom visits, and assemblies. Jill loves reading to students, and she speaks on topics such as bullying, underage drinking, and drug use, and inclusion. Jill also speaks about writing topics, and her experiences as a writer.

For information about the author or her books, visit jillvanderwood.com

To contact Jill Vanderwood

email brightonsbooks@gmail.com

Include 'Bring an Author to My School' in your subject line when emailing.

Please include your name (at least your first name), school, and the city and state you live in. Also include the name of your principal or a contact person, and a contact phone number.

Be Kind! Kids Can Make A Difference

In the Unkindness Club story, Purdy and Rowen started their own Kindness Club. They got the school involved and, with the support of local businesses, held a **Be My Neighbor Party:** Admission—one blanket for a homeless pet, an infant, or an elderly person. The quilt club also donated special quilts for veterans.

These are some of the ideas Purdy and Rowen used to teach kindness and to help get the community involved:

- The Library had a signup sheet for a story time volunteer to read and do crafts with kids.

- There was a signup sheet for pine cone pickup in parks and cemeteries.

- The quilt club offered grab-and-go quilt kits for volunteers to piece and tie quilts at home.

- A nursing home and hospital requested help with snow removal during the winter months.

- Schools and churches needed Spanish translators.

- A church pastor requested a volunteer ASL sign language interpreter for church services.

- A signup sheet was also set up for volunteers to stock books for the Little Free Library.

- S.A.C.K—Supporting a Community with Kindness—needed volunteers to knit or crochet soap sacks and add a bar of soap for homeless shelters.

- Volunteers were also requested at an animal shelter to foster pets, walk dogs, create gift bags for pet adopters, and participate in a Read-to-a-Pet reading program. The reader must be at least six years old and anyone under ten needed to bring a parent with them.

For more information on how you can help in your community go to Justserve.org.

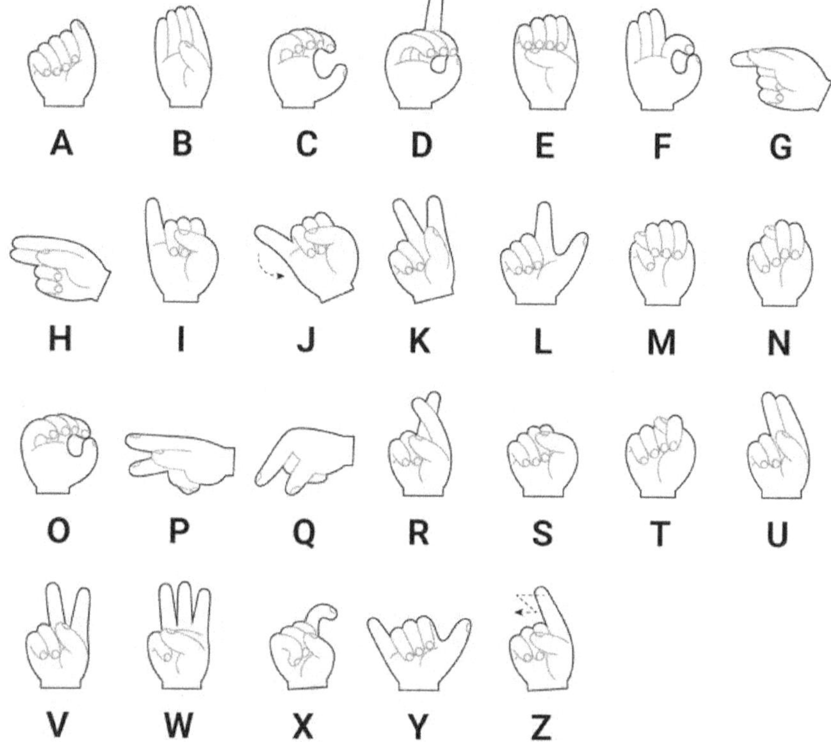

A
B
C
D
E
F
G
H
I
J
K
L
M
N
O
P
Q
R
S
T
U
V
W
X
Y
Z